The Number *After* You

By

Rosanne Baker

www.copperlightpress.com

The Number After You
Copyright © 2025 by Rosanne Baker
All rights reserved.

This is a work of fiction. Names, characters, places, and incidents are products of the author's imagination or are used fictitiously. Any resemblance to actual events, locales, or persons, living or dead, is entirely coincidental.

Published by Copper Light Press
CopperLightPress.com
ISBN: 979-8-9936451-0-0
First Edition

Table of Contents

Contents

PROLOGUE: Road Trip

The car smelled of gas station coffee, a strawberry air freshener dangling from the rear-view mirror, and the cinnamon gum Sheridan always chewed when she was nervous about exams. Jenna's music streamed from her phone, wedged in a cup holder, and connected to the car's beat-up stereo through an auxiliary cord that crackled whenever they hit a bump.

"Turn it up!" Lily called from the back seat, tearing open a package of powdered donuts she'd grabbed from the vending machine during their last stop. "This is my favorite song!"

The opening piano of "Dancing Queen" filled the small car, and all three girls immediately started singing along, their voices overlapping in the kind of chaotic harmony that only comes from years of friendship and zero shame about singing ability.

"Anybody could be that guy!" Jenna belted, tapping her fingers on the steering wheel with theatrical intensity.

Lily joined in, a little off-key. "Night is young and the music's high!"

Sheridan doubled over laughing, nearly choking on her donut. "You guys are awful singers!"

"Says the girl who got kicked out of choir in eighth grade," Jenna shot back.

"That was your fault!" Sheridan protested. "You made me laugh during the concert!"

"Eleven years later, and you're still blaming me," Jenna said, grinning at Lily in the rear-view mirror.

"She's been like this since second grade."

"And you've been getting me in trouble since second grade," Lily said fondly.

The song changed to another Taylor Swift track. It was always Taylor Swift when Jenna was in charge of the playlist and Sheridan reached into the bag of road-trip snacks between her feet.

"Okay, inventory check: chips, donuts, and gummy bears so old they should have a pension."

"The donuts aren't an obsession," Lily said, already reaching forward to grab the bag. "They're a lifestyle choice."

"You bought three bags at the gas station," Jenna pointed out.

"Two were for my mom. She loves these things." Lily shifted in her seat. The words came out lightly, but guilt pricked at her. She'd meant to drive home last weekend and got two busy to make the trip.

"Can't believe we've been in the apartment over a year, and I still forget to bring her stuff from La Crosse."

Sheridan perked up. "Remember move-in day? We thought we were so grown up."

"We are grown-ups," Jenna said. "We pay rent. We have a spice rack."

"That Lily alphabetized," Sheridan added.

"And you two put that song on backward just to torture me," Lily said. Her phone buzzed, and she pulled it out to find another photo from Hope.

"Your mom is literally the best cook," Sheridan sighed. "My mom thinks reheating Chinese takeout counts as home cooking."

"Your mom works night shifts at the hospital," Lily said loyally. "She's saving lives. Cooking is optional when you're a hero."

"Still, those breadsticks look like heaven." Sheridan popped a gummy bear into her mouth and made a face. "Okay, these are definitely stale. Why didn't we throw them away at the last stop?"

"Because you have a compulsive need to finish every bag of candy you start," Jenna said. "It's like a disorder."

"It's called being responsible! Do you know how many children are starving in…"

"Children who would not want your stale gummy bears," Lily interrupted, stealing a donut. "Just admit you have no self-control and move on."

The rain had started about an hour ago, light at first, just enough to make the windshield sparkle. Now it came down harder, the drops fat and heavy, drumming against the roof with growing insistence. The wipers beat a steady rhythm across the glass as the oncoming headlights blurred into impressionist smears of white and yellow.

"Weather's getting nasty," Jenna said, leaning forward slightly to peer through the windshield. She turned down the music a notch. "Maybe we should've left earlier."

"We left when we always leave," Lily said, though she noticed the tension in Jenna's jaw, the way her knuckles whitened on the wheel. Jenna hid anxiety behind control—it was her default. Lily wanted to say something soothing but didn't want to sound like a child offering reassurance to a parent.

"GPS still says we'll be there by eight. Mom's not expecting us until eight-thirty anyway."

"I just hate driving in the rain," Jenna muttered, both hands tight on the wheel now. "Can't see anything. Other drivers are idiots in weather like this."

"Want me to drive?" Sheridan offered. "I've driven in worse."

"No, I'm fine. Just… maybe less singing for a bit? So I can concentrate?"

The car fell into a subdued quiet, though Lily could see Sheridan still mouthing the words to the Taylor Swift song playing softly in the background.

Outside, the Wisconsin farmland stretched in all directions, fields of harvested corn stubble and bare earth fading into gray dusk. Farmhouses dotted the landscape, their windows glowing yellow and warm. Lily's gaze followed one, then another—tiny pockets of safety in a darkening world. She imagined her mom inside one of them, dinner simmering, lights low, waiting. The thought filled her chest and tightened it all at once.

Lily pulled her feet up and wrapped her arms around them. This was her favorite part of any trip home: the last hour when anticipation built like pressure in her chest. Soon she'd be walking through the front door of her childhood home, breathing in the smell of whatever amazing thing her mom had been cooking all day, falling back into the comfortable rhythms of the house that had shaped her.

She pictured Hope standing at the counter in her paint-stained sweatshirt, humming to herself, pretending not to check the clock every five minutes. Lily should've texted earlier. Should've told her she loved her outright, not just with emojis. She always thought there'd be time for another message, another visit.

"Oh," she said suddenly, remembering the conversation she'd been meaning to have. She pulled out her phone and started typing as she talked, the way teenagers do—carrying on multiple conversations across multiple platforms at once. "Mom, there's this bookstore owner I think you'd really like."

"Yeah?" Sheridan perked up, always interested in Lily's romantic life, even though this clearly wasn't about romance. "College professor? Grad student?"

"He's older. Like Dad's age, maybe older. Sam. He owns the bookstore near campus, Turner's Books. Remember, I started going there in my freshman year, and he's just… he gets it, you know? Books, life, everything."

"Your mom would love that," Jenna said. "She always says she misses having someone to trade book recommendations with."

"That's exactly what I was thinking." Lily's thumbs flew across her phone screen. "He gave me this book last week, *The Seven Husbands of Evelyn Hugo*, and when I told him I'd already read it, he said, 'Well, then you can tell me if I should bother with the other six husbands or if the first one covers all the important material.'"

"Okay, that's actually pretty funny," Sheridan admitted.

"Your mom seems pretty content to me," she added gently. "She's got her work, her garden, her book club..."

"Easy for you to say," Lily teased. "Your parents are still disgustingly in love. Mine have been divorced since I was seven."

"My parents ask about you like you're their kid," Sheridan said. "Perks of living next door to you your whole life."

"I know, but it's different..." She didn't finish. Some thoughts were too complicated to untangle in a moving car, especially with rain blurring the world outside.

The car fell quiet for a moment. All three girls had watched Hope rebuild herself after the divorce, had seen her struggle with confidence and then slowly, carefully, reclaim her life on her own terms. It had been inspiring and heartbreaking in equal measure.

"Well," Jenna said finally, "if anyone could convince your mom she's worth loving, it'd be a bookstore owner with a sense of humor."

"Exactly." Lily grinned and held up her phone to show them Hope's quick reply: Can't wait to hear about him! Drive safe, girls. See you soon.

"She says drive safe," Lily announced, settling back into her seat with satisfaction. "I'm going to invite Sam to the reading the campus bookstore's doing next month. Mom said she might come to that."

"Subtle," Jenna said dryly.

"I prefer 'strategic,'" Lily replied, typing back: Jenna's driving like someone's grandmother. Sheridan's already asleep. We'll be there soon. Love you. 🌸

The flower emoji had been theirs since Lily's first phone, her mother's nickname for her: *my little flower*. It used to embarrass her; now it felt like a charm she wore openly.

The music shifted to something slower, an indie folk song with a guitar that sounded like rainfall. Outside, darkness had swallowed the farmland entirely, the November evening reducing the world to a ribbon of highway stretching through the void, punctuated only by the glow of distant farmhouse windows.

"This song makes me sleepy," Sheridan murmured, leaning her head against the window.

"Don't actually fall asleep," Jenna warned. "I need someone to keep me awake. This rain is hypnotic."

It was coming down harder now. Jenna had slowed the car, both hands gripping the wheel, her knuckles pale in the dashboard's glow.

"You're doing great," Lily said softly, noticing her friend's tension. She wanted to reach forward, to rest a hand on Jenna's shoulder, to say everything was okay—but the words stayed behind her teeth.

"I know. I just hate not being able to see clearly."

As if summoned by her words, a truck roared past them in the opposite direction, too fast for the conditions, its spray of water momentarily blinding them. Jenna cursed under her breath and eased off the gas even more.

"Idiot," Sheridan muttered.

"Twenty more minutes," Lily said, checking the GPS. "Then we'll be eating Mom's cooking and complaining about how much homework we have to do over break."

"Your mom's going to ask about our love lives," Jenna predicted. "She always does. What am I going to tell her this time?"

"The truth?" Sheridan suggested. "That you're too busy with your double major to date anyone and that's perfectly fine."

"She's going to think I'm sad and pathetic."

"You're neither," Lily said firmly. "You're focused. There's a difference."

"What about you?" Sheridan asked, turning to look at Lily in the back seat. "Any romantic developments I should know about? Anyone new hanging around the bookstore?"

"Just Sam, the owner, and he's not a romantic development," Lily said as she slid her phone in her purse.

The lights of a distant farmhouse blurred into star-like points through the rain, creating an impressionist painting across the glass. She was about to post it to her Instagram story with a caption about coming home when something made her look up.

Headlights. Coming straight at them, in their lane.

For a moment, Lily's brain couldn't process what she was seeing. That couldn't be right. Cars didn't drive in the wrong lane. The dotted yellow line existed for a reason. It had to be a trick of the rain, or the angle of the road, or—

"Jenna," she said, her voice strangely calm.

"I see it," Jenna replied, her knuckles white on the steering wheel.

The headlights grew brighter. Closer. No mistake now.

"JENNA!" Sheridan screamed.

Time thickened, moving like honey. Lily watched Jenna yank the wheel hard right, watched the speedometer needle swing as the car careened off the highway. Sheridan's hands flew up to brace against the dashboard. Lily felt her purse slip from her fingers and heard it hit the floor with a sharp thud that sounded too loud for the world.

The car tilted. Spun. Lifted off the ground.

In that suspended second before impact, Lily thought about her unsent message still glowing on the screen: Almost home. Can't wait to see you, Mom. Your little flower.

Then the world exploded.

Metal screamed. Glass shattered in a symphony of destruction. The car rolled once, twice, physics taking over where human control had ended. Lily's body slammed against the door, then the ceiling, then the other door, her seat belt the only thing keeping her from being thrown clear.

She heard Sheridan's scream cut off. Jenna's sharp gasp. The terrible crunch of the frame compacting around them like a closing fist.

Headlights still blazed from the pickup truck in the road, flooding the wreck with harsh white light. The driver's door opened slowly with a long, metallic groan.

A man stumbled out.

Mid-thirties, maybe. Ball cap pulled low, soaked instantly by the rain. His boots slapped against the pavement as he staggered forward, swearing under his breath. His movements were clumsy, unsteady — panic mixed with something else, something sluggish, like his body wasn't fully under his control.

He stopped short at the sight of the mangled car, his chest heaving. "Oh Jesus… oh God…" His voice cracked.

He rushed to the driver's side first, yanking at the door. It didn't budge, crushed into the frame. Jenna flinched when she saw him, blood streaking her face.

"Please…help us," she rasped, reaching a trembling hand toward him.

He froze. His eyes darted to her, then away. He let go of the handle like it had burned him. "I…"

Sheridan tried to push herself up despite the searing agony in her leg. "Call someone! Please! She's not, she's not waking up…" Her voice broke, high and frantic.

The man cursed, stepping back, glancing wildly down the road as if hoping someone else would appear, someone who actually knew what to do. No one came. Only rain. Only trees bending in the wind.

He swore again and stumbled toward the back door. Yanked it open.

And there she was.

Lily slumped sideways, unconscious, her head lolling against the seatbelt. Rain blew in through the open door, plastering her hair to her cheek, streaking her blood down across her jaw.

The man froze, breath shaking, his face pale under the wash of his headlights.

Then, in the dim glow of the interior light, he saw it.

Something silver, glinting faintly on the floorboard beneath her feet.

A purse. The strap twisted like a snake. Her phone half-slid from the zipper, screen cracked but faintly lit with the ghost of a notification.

His chest heaved. His hands shook. For a long second he stood there, caught between terror and instinct, staring at the broken girl in the seat and the glittering object at her feet.

Behind him, Sheridan whimpered. Jenna coughed, choking.

The man muttered something under his breath — a string of curses, or maybe a prayer.

Then he reached down, snatched the purse, and clutched it to his chest.

Lily's head shifted slightly with the motion, her lips parting in the faintest breath, but he didn't notice. Or he refused to.

He staggered backward, boots slipping in the mud at the roadside. The purse strap swung as he ran.

"Wait!" Sheridan screamed, her voice cracking in despair. "Don't…please…"

But he was already climbing back into his truck, slamming the door so hard the frame rattled. The engine roared to life, tires spinning, gravel and rain spraying behind him.

The headlights swung wide, then receded down the dark curve of the highway, shrinking to two pale dots swallowed by the storm

Then silence.

Steam hissed from the crumpled hood. Rain drummed on the overturned car. A single clap of thunder rolled through the distance. Inside the wreckage, everything stilled.

Lily's last thought was of the breadsticks waiting in her mother's kitchen, golden and warm beneath their checkered cloth, and how she would never taste them again.

CHAPTER 1: Six Months Later

May

Hope woke to birdsong that felt like an accusation.

The house had been too quiet for six months. No music bleeding through the ceiling. No footsteps on the stairs. No midnight texts lighting up her phone with random thoughts about the universe, requests for book recommendations, or photos of terrible dorm food captioned, Miss your cooking.

She sat up slowly, the way you do when your body has forgotten how to want the day. The clock read 7:23 a.m. early for a Saturday, but sleep had become unreliable. A friend who arrived uninvited stayed too long or not long enough, then left without saying goodbye.

Today was May eleventh.

Lily would've been twenty-one.

Hope pressed her fingers against her eyes until stars bloomed. Breathing hurt. Existing hurt. But she'd learned over the past six months that pain was just another task on the list like brushing teeth, answering emails, or pretending to care about manuscript deadlines.

She pulled on the same jeans as yesterday, the same cream sweater that smelled faintly of the lavender sachets Rebecca had tucked into her drawers during her last visit. For calm, Rebecca had said as if a drawer could be calm, as if Hope could borrow serenity from dried flowers.

Downstairs, the kitchen held its usual morning geometry: coffeepot, mug, spoon. The refrigerator hummed its one-note song. Outside, Mrs. Chen's cat picked its way across the dewy lawn with the slow dignity of someone who had places to be.

Hope made coffee because that's what you did. The ritual steadied her hands: grind the beans, measure the water, wait for the machine to hiss, and drip and fill the house with a smell that still meant morning even when morning felt like a lie.

While it brewed, she opened her laptop at the kitchen table. Three manuscripts waited for her editorial notes. She'd been working from home as a freelance editor for a small publishing house for nearly fifteen years, since Lily was in kindergarten. The job had fit around school drop-offs, sick days, and soccer games. After the divorce, it became a lifeline, a steady income, flexible hours, a reason to stay tethered to language when her own words had stopped coming.

She'd always loved the work: the puzzle of making a sentence sing, the satisfaction of helping a writer find their truest voice. But since November, the manuscripts felt like relics from another world. She read them. She made notes. She sent them back. But the joy had leaked out somewhere, pooled on a highway shoulder beside shattered glass and twisted metal.

Still, she opened the first file. Read the first page. Made a note about passive voice, something to do with her hands.

The coffee finished. She poured a cup, black, no sugar. Lily used to tease her: How do you drink that? It tastes like punishment. Hope would laugh and say, you'll understand when you're older.

But Lily would never be older than twenty.

Hope set the mug down too hard. Coffee sloshed onto the manuscript printout, blooming brown across a paragraph about a woman learning to live alone after loss. Of course. The universe had a sense of irony, cruel and perfectly timed.

She blotted the pages with a dish towel, then gave up on editing.

Instead, she did what she'd been avoiding since she woke up: she climbed the stairs to Lily's room.

The door creaked, just as it always had, with a familiar sound that once meant Lily was home from school, awake, or sneaking out to meet friends. Now, it signified something else entirely: Hope was entering a shrine.

She'd kept everything exactly as Lily had left it that final morning in November, the day before Thanksgiving break, the day before everything fell apart.

The bed was unmade (Lily never made her bed; it had been one of their ongoing battles). Textbooks sat stacked on the desk beside a half-empty can of Diet Coke and an open bag of sour gummy worms.

On the desk sat a small wooden box labeled Quote Collection in Lily's looping handwriting. Hope opened it carefully. Inside were index cards covered in Lily's script quotes copied from books she loved:

"We read to know we're not alone." C.S. Lewis

"There is no greater agony than bearing an untold story inside you." Maya Angelou

"A reader lives a thousand lives before he dies. The man who never reads lives only one." George R.R. Martin

At the bottom of the box lay a sticky note: For Book Rescue – leave these in books for people who need them.

Hope pressed one of the cards against her chest. Even Lily's handwriting felt like an act of care.

Book Rescue Lily's project, her dream of creating a lending library filled with books that saved lives.

Jenna had explained it through tears at the funeral: Lily wanted to leave books in the student center with notes tucked inside for anyone who needed them. No checkout system. Just take what you need. Leave a message for the next person, like bottles tossed into the ocean for drowning students.

They'd never got to start it. Lily had been collecting books, writing notes, and making plans. And then she was gone.

Hope sat on the edge of the unmade bed and pulled Lily's quilt around her shoulders. It still smelled like her shampoo, something floral and bright that Hope had started buying in bulk because Lily went through a bottle every two weeks. She breathed it in, held it, and let it go.

On the nightstand, Lily's phone charger lay coiled like a sleeping snake. The phone itself was still gone in police evidence somewhere; they had said it was recovered from the drunk driver's car after he fled the scene.

In those first terrible weeks, she'd tried texting the number. Desperate, irrational messages sent into the void.

Are you still with me, my little flower?

I can't do this without you.

The house is too quiet.

I made your favorite coffee. It tastes like nothing.

All blue bubbles. No gray replies.

Rebecca had handled all the awful administrative details of death while Hope moved through the house like a ghost.

The phone company, the bank, the university, and the insurance company.

Rebecca had made lists, calls, and held Hope's hand as she signed forms she didn't even read.

Hope usually nodded without really understanding. Nothing had made sense then, and nothing did now.

She pulled her phone from her pocket, her constant companion, her lifeline to the world.

Scrolling to Lily's contact, she opened their messages. The last text was still there, sent at 7:47 p.m. on November 22.

Jenna's driving like someone's grandmother. Sheridan's already asleep. We'll be there soon. Love you. ✿

The flower emoji.

It had been their thing since Lily got her first phone. My little flower, Hope used to call her when she was small.

It had started as a joke. Lily had insisted on being a flower for Halloween when she was four, and Hope had sewn an elaborate costume with petals and leaves. The nickname stuck.

By high school, Lily would roll her eyes at it but never asked Hope to stop. The flower emoji had become their quiet shorthand for love: *I love you. I'm safe. Don't worry.*

Hope's thumb hovered over the keyboard.

She'd stopped texting the number months ago. It had become painfully pointless, a quiet kind of self-harm she couldn't justify, even in her worst moments.

But today, on Lily's birthday, in her room, wrapped in her quilt, breathing in the scent of her shampoo, the urge returned like muscle memory.

Hope typed before she could think better of it:

Happy birthday, baby. I miss you so much.

She hit send.

The message turned blue and sat there delivered into the void, another bottle tossed into an empty ocean.

Hope set the phone on the nightstand and pulled the quilt tighter around her.

Outside, a lawnmower started up somewhere down the block. Life is going on. The world is spinning. The universe is expanding.

None of it cared that Lily Hawthorne should have been twenty-one today, that she would have wanted chocolate cake and Thai food and a terrible comedy on Netflix; that she would have texted Hope seventeen times with random thoughts and made her laugh until her stomach hurt.

The room blurred. Hope let the tears come. Six months had taught her not to fight them; they came when they wanted, left when they were done, and resistance only made it hurt more.

She was crying into Lily's pillow when her phone buzzed.

At first, she thought it was Rebecca, her sister, who checked in constantly, called every few days, and sent articles about grief and healing that Hope never read.

Or maybe Jenna or Sheridan. They texted sometimes, careful messages asking how she was, sharing memories of Lily, trying to stay connected through the same loss.

But when Hope picked up the phone, her heart stopped.

A gray bubble.

A new message.

From Lily's old number.

I'm so sorry you have to go through this.

Hope's hands shook so hard she almost dropped the phone.

She stared at the screen, waiting for the words to shift into something that made sense, something possible, something that didn't break every law of physics, death, and cellular service.

But the message didn't change. It stayed.

I'm so sorry you have to go through this.

Her mind raced.

Rebecca had canceled the line. Months ago. Hope had been there, had heard the hold music, had watched Rebecca write down confirmation numbers and dates. The account was closed. The number was dead.

Except it wasn't.

Someone had answered.

Someone was on the other end.

Hope's breath came short and fast. Her vision tunneled. The room tilted.

She thought about the articles she'd read late at night when sleep wouldn't come, stories about signs from beyond, messages from the dead, technology as a bridge between worlds. Her book club friend swore her mother sent cardinals. A woman in her grief support group said her husband's favorite song would play at just the right moments. People talked about pennies and feathers and numbers on clocks, dreams that felt too real to be only dreams.

What if.

What if grief had frequencies the living couldn't explain?

What if love found ways?

What if Lily...

Hope's fingers moved before she could stop them.

Lily? Is this really you?

She hit send and immediately wished she could take it back.

She sounded insane. She sounded desperate. She sounded like a woman who'd lost her only child and was grasping for anything that looked like a rope in the dark.

But the message was sent.

Hope held her breath. Counted to ten. Twenty. Thirty.

Then the phone buzzed.

I'm here. I'm listening.

A sound tore from Hope's throat, half sob, half laugh, all unhinged.

She pressed the phone to her chest as if it might slip away.

Her whole-body shook.

I'm here.

Someone was there.

Someone was listening.

Whether it was Lily's spirit, a stranger's kindness, or her own mind splintering into pieces just sane enough to comfort her, Hope didn't care. Not right now. Not today.

She began to type, her fingers trembling.

I don't know how to do this. How to have birthdays without you. How to be in the world when you're not in it.

The response came quickly:

Tell me what you're missing today.

And so Hope did.

She curled up on Lily's bed, wrapped in her daughter's quilt, and began to type everything the chocolate cake Lily loved, the Thai food tradition they'd started when she turned sixteen, the terrible comedies they'd watched until their stomachs hurt from laughing.

She wrote about Lily's love of books and music, and her two best friends. She wrote about the apartment in La Crosse where Lily had finally gotten to live with Jenna and Sheridan, how excited she'd been to have her own space, but how she still called all the time, how they texted about everything and nothing.

She wrote about the divorce when Lily was seven, how David had left for Minneapolis, for his new life and new family, how Lily had once asked if it was her fault, and how Hope had held her and promised it wasn't. That some people just weren't meant to stay.

She wrote about how Lily had become her whole world, maybe too much, maybe unhealthily so, but after David left, it had been just the two of them in the yellow Victorian house. They'd made it enough. More than enough.

And the messages came back steady, gentle.

She sounds wonderful. You must miss her terribly. It's okay to take a break. Grief doesn't ask permission.

Hope wrote until her fingers ached until the light through Lily's window turned gold, then gray until she'd poured out six months of held breath and swallowed screams.

When she finally stopped, her phone showed seventeen blue bubbles and seventeen gray.

A conversation with someone who listened without fixing, who let her be broken without trying to glue the pieces back together.

Hope didn't know who was on the other end. Part of her desperately wanted it to be Lily reaching back across whatever divide still separated them.

Part of her knew it was probably someone else. Someone kind. Someone who'd been assigned Lily's old number and had chosen to comfort a grieving stranger instead of blocking her.

She began to type:

Who are you?

The answer came after a long pause:

Someone who understands what it's like to lose someone. Someone who wants to help if I can.

Hope stared at the words.

Not, *I'm Lily.*

Not, *I'm texting from heaven.*

Just: *Someone who understands.*

The rational part of her brain recognized this as a stranger, a reassigned number, a coincidence that only felt like fate because grief made you desperate for patterns, for meaning, for any proof that the universe wasn't just chaos and accidents and drunk drivers on rainy highways.

But the part of her that had been drowning for six months, the part that woke up every morning to an empty house and went to bed every night in sheets that felt too big, that part didn't care about rational.

That part needed this.

Thank you for talking to me, Hope typed. *Whoever you are.*

Always came back. *I'm here whenever you need.*

Hope closed her eyes and let herself believe not that it was Lily, exactly, but that maybe love did find ways.

Maybe grief broke the rules.

Maybe sometimes strangers were angels, or angels were strangers, and maybe it didn't matter which, because the result was the same: someone had answered when she called into the void.

She fell asleep like that, on Lily's bed, phone clutched to her chest, the gray bubbles still glowing softly in the darkening room.

When Hope woke, it was fully dark outside. The clock read 9:47 p.m. She'd slept for hours, the first real sleep in days.

She sat up slowly, disoriented. Her phone battery was at fifteen percent. The message thread was still open.

For a moment, she wondered if she'd dreamed it. But no, the messages were there. Blue and gray. A conversation with someone who'd let her spill her grief into the electronic void.

Hope scrolled back through what she'd written and felt her cheeks heat. She'd told a stranger everything—about Lily, about David, about being alone, about texting a dead girl's number like some kind of grief-crazed Victorian spiritualist.

But the stranger had been kind.

That was the thing she kept coming back to.

Whoever had Lily's number, whoever had answered her desperate birthday text, they'd been kind. They'd listened. They'd responded with gentleness, patience, and understanding.

Maybe that was enough.

Maybe that was everything.

Hope plugged her phone into the charger on Lily's nightstand and stood on shaky legs. She needed to eat something. Rebecca would be proud she'd been harping about nutrition, about routine, about the small acts of self-care that kept you tethered to living.

Downstairs, the kitchen was dark. Hope turned on the light and blinked at the brightness. The coffee she'd made that morning sat cold in the pot. The manuscript pages, still coffee-stained, lay scattered across the table.

She made toast because it was easy. Buttered it because Rebecca's voice in her head said *Protein, Hope, you need protein.* She ate standing at the counter, looking out the window at the dark street.

The house felt different. Lighter, maybe. Or maybe it was her wrung out, emptied, but somehow still standing.

Her phone buzzed upstairs.

Hope set down the toast and climbed the steps back to Lily's room.

A new message waited on the screen, glowing softly in the dark.

I hope you're taking care of yourself. Eating something. Resting. Tomorrow is another day to miss her, and another day you survived missing her.

Hope's throat tightened.

She typed: *I made toast. It counts.*

The response was immediate: *It counts. Small steps are still steps.*

Hope sat on the edge of Lily's bed and felt something shift in her chest, not healing, exactly, but maybe the first small movement after six months of paralysis.

Good night, she typed. *Thank you for today. It helped.*

Good night. I'm here.

Hope set the phone on the nightstand and looked around Lily's room, the unmade bed, the scattered textbooks, the sticky notes that would never come down.

A life interrupted. A future canceled. A space where a daughter should be.

The grief was still there. It always would be.

But for the first time in six months, Hope felt like she could breathe within it.

She stood, turned off the light, and left the door open a crack, the way she used to when Lily was small and afraid of the dark.

In her own room, Hope crawled under the covers without changing. Hope closed her eyes and let herself imagine just for tonight that somewhere in the universe, Lily was okay. That death wasn't an ending but a passage. That love could still whisper I'm here across the unbridgeable distance between life and whatever came after.

She didn't quite believe it.

But she wanted to.

And maybe, for now, wanting was enough.

CHAPTER 2: The Number

May 11, La Crosse

Sam Turner woke at six-thirty to the sound of rain against his apartment window, a soft, persistent tapping that reminded him of Elise's fingers on a keyboard when she was deep in thought.

He lay still for a moment, listening, letting the memory wash over him without trying to chase it.

Two years, three months, and sixteen days since she'd died.

Not that he was counting.

(He was always counting.)

He pushed back the covers and set his feet on the cold hardwood floor. The apartment was sparse: a bed, a dresser, a bookshelf, and a chair, everything necessary, nothing extra.

After Elise died, he'd gotten rid of most of it: the decorative pillows she'd loved, the throw blankets, the framed prints of Paris and Dublin and all the places they'd planned to visit after the bookstore was established, after her treatment was done. After, after, after.

Turns out there was no after.

Sam showered, dressed in jeans and the same navy Henley he wore most days, then made coffee in the French press Elise had insisted made better coffee than any machine.

She'd been right. She was usually right.

He ate toast standing at the counter, watching the gray morning settle over the city. La Crosse was just waking up, a few cars on the street, a jogger in reflective gear, the bakery across the way flicking on its lights.

Sunday morning. The store would be quiet. Most students are sleeping off Saturday night, the town moving at half speed.

He liked it that way.

Turner's Books sat on a corner lot in a brick building that leaned slightly west, as if drawn toward the river's pull. The hand-painted sign above the door read, in green letters on white:

TURNER'S BOOKS – NEW, USED, AND NECESSARY.

Necessary. That had been Elise's addition.

"Books aren't a luxury," she'd said when they were painting the sign together during her last good month. "They're oxygen. Put necessary on there so people know we mean it."

Sam let himself in through the service door. The smell hit him immediately: old paper, dust, yesterday's coffee, and the faint sweetness of a cinnamon candle burned too long. It was the smell of every bookstore he'd ever loved, and it steadied him the way nothing else could.

He moved through the space by habit: lights on, heat adjusted, classical station on low, Elise's rule: nothing with lyrics before nine a.m., cash drawer counted, door unlocked, sign flipped to OPEN.

The first floor held new releases, bestsellers, and general fiction. Worn rugs softened the scarred wood floors. Mismatched armchairs clustered near the front window. The counter, original to the building, was thick oak, marked with decades of dings and coffee rings that no refinishing could erase.

Sam liked those marks. Proof that something could be both useful and beautiful.

Upstairs felt different, quieter, more intimate. Poetry. Literary fiction. Classics. And the nook.

The nook was why students loved this place: a leather armchair by the west-facing window, afternoon light spilling in, a small table just big enough for a laptop and coffee, a green-shaded lamp, and a view of the street below, enough movement to feel connected, enough calm to think.

Lily Hawthorne's spot.

Sam climbed the stairs and paused at the top, looking at the empty chair. He could still see her there, legs tucked under, Diet Coke sweating on the table, head bent over a book, fingers absently twisting a strand of dark hair.

She'd been coming since the start of her sophomore year, about eighteen months ago. Quiet. Polite. The kind of shy that wasn't fragile but deliberate, careful about who got her words.

But she'd talked to him.

Not at first. At first, she only browsed, bought books, and offered a small nod when he rang her up. But over the weeks, then months, she began asking his opinion.

Have you read this? What did you think? Would you recommend the sequel?

And then, one afternoon, when the store was empty and Sam was shelving returns upstairs, she'd said, "Can I ask you something?"

"Of course."

"Why keep this place open? I mean, Amazon exists. E-books exist. Most bookstores are dying." She'd said it without judgment, just genuine curiosity.

Sam set down the stack of books and considered. "My wife wanted a bookstore," he said finally. "Before she died, we bought this place together. Kept it open during her treatment. She said books were proof that beauty could be held in your hands. I keep it open because she was right."

Lily had been quiet for a moment. Then she said softly, "That's the most romantic thing I've ever heard."

Sam laughed, actually laughed, surprising himself. "Don't tell anyone. I have a reputation for being curmudgeonly."

"Your secret's safe with me."

After that, they talked more. Nothing heavy books, mostly. The weather. Her classes. His recommendations. She'd told him about her roommates, Jenna and Sheridan, best friends since childhood, and about the apartment they'd finally gotten together. Her mom is back home, who worried too much, but in a good way.

She'd mentioned her major: English, with dreams of doing something with books, though she wasn't sure what yet. She'd talked about her project, Book Rescue, with the kind of passion that reminded Sam why he'd wanted to work with books in the first place.

But what he remembered most were the quotes.

Lily left them tucked inside books, index cards in looping handwriting, each one carefully chosen, always relevant to the book, the section, or the person who might need it.

Sam found the first one inside a Mary Oliver poetry collection:

"Tell me, what is it you plan to do with your one wild and precious life?" - Mary Oliver

He'd shown it to Lily the next time she came in. "Did you leave this?"

She'd blushed. "Yeah. Sorry, is that weird? I can stop…"

"Don't stop," he said. "It's perfect."

After that, he started finding them everywhere in grief memoirs, fantasy novels, and even self-help books. Students began looking for them, calling them Lily drops. Some collected them. Others left the cards where they were, understanding that each quote was meant to find its next person.

"I'm practicing," Lily explained once. "For Book Rescue. Trying to figure out which words help. Sometimes the right quote at the right time can…"

"Save someone," Sam finished.

"Yeah." She smiled. "Save someone."

The last quote he found from her was tucked inside a Kent Haruf novel, the week before Thanksgiving. Before the crash. Before everything ended.

"You have to remember that goodness is more powerful than evil. . . And that love is stronger than hate." - Kent Haruf.

Sam had kept that card. It was downstairs now, folded neatly in the register drawer beside the spare keys and emergency cash. He read it sometimes when the store was empty and the grief felt too big.

He'd needed it often in December.

Sam learned about the crash from a student.

The Monday after Thanksgiving, a girl came in with red-rimmed eyes and asked for "something to read when you lose someone suddenly."

"Joan Didion," Sam had said automatically. "*The Year of Magical Thinking*. It's honest without being cruel."

"Thank you." She hesitated. "There was an accident. Highway 23. Three girls from the campus. One of them… Lily Hawthorne used to come here, right?"

Sam's hand froze on the register. "Lily?"

"She left those quote cards in books. Everyone loved them." The girl's voice cracked. "She died. Her roommates survived, but she… she didn't make it.

Sam sat down.

The girl paid and left quietly. Sam sat behind the counter for twenty minutes, unable to move. Then he climbed the stairs, sank into Lily's chair, and stared out the window at the ordinary street where ordinary people did ordinary things, unaware that the world had just become smaller and darker.

He went to the funeral. Stood in the back and introduced himself to no one. He watched as two girls with bandages, Jenna and Sheridan, had to stand at the front and talk about their friend through tears. He watched a woman in the front row, Lily's mother, obviously, with the same dark hair, the same quiet intensity, hold herself together with visible effort.

He wanted to say something to tell the mother that her daughter had made his bookstore better, that she'd left words in books that helped strangers, that she'd talked about her mom with love and worry and the kind of fierce protectiveness you only give to people who've been hurt.

But it didn't feel like his place. He was just the bookstore owner, one of dozens of people Lily had touched in her short life.

So he slipped out before anyone could ask who he was, drove back to Turner's, sat in the dark, and let himself grieve for a girl who'd reminded him that goodness still existed in the world.

Now, standing in the empty upstairs on a gray Sunday morning in May, Sam touched the back of the leather chair and whispered, "Happy birthday, Lily."

She would have been twenty-one today.

He'd thought about her all week, knowing the date was coming. He thought about texting her mother, but he didn't have her number, didn't know her name beyond "Hope," and wasn't even sure she'd remember him from the memorial.

So he did what he always did: opened the store, shelved books, helped customers, and carried the grief privately.

Downstairs, the bell over the door chimed.

Sam descended the stairs to find a young man browsing the new releases, hood up, headphones in. Sam nodded at him and went behind the counter.

His phone sat on the shelf below the register, a new phone from last month, after the old one finally died. He'd resisted for weeks; the old phone held Elise's voicemails, Elise's texts, the last photo she'd sent of the bookstore sign with the caption Our dream in green letters, but the battery wouldn't hold a charge anymore. Eventually, even grief had to bow to practicality.

The new phone felt wrong. Too light. Too smooth. Nothing about it knew him yet.

It buzzed a text notification.

Sam picked it up, expecting spam or maybe Bill from the used-book warehouse confirming Tuesday's delivery.

Instead:

Happy birthday, baby. I miss you so much.

Wrong number.

Obviously, a wrong number, the message meant for someone else, someone named baby, someone whose birthday was today…

Sam's stomach dropped.

Today.

May eleventh.

Lily's birthday.

His hands went cold.

Baby. That's what mothers called daughters, wasn't it? The kind of endearment that lingered even when the child was grown.

The phone suddenly felt heavy. Dangerous. Like something that could detonate if he touched it wrong.

He should ignore it. Delete it. Block the number.

But.

He thought about the woman at the funeral, folded in on herself like a paper crane, holding her grief together with trembling hands.

He thought about Lily talking about her mom with such love. *She worries, but in a good way. She's been alone since the divorce. I'm all she has.*

He thought about his own grief, two years of it now still sharp enough to draw blood on bad days. About how desperate he'd been for any sign that Elise was still somewhere, somehow. How he'd reread her favorite books, searching for hidden messages. How he'd played her voicemail just to hear her voice, again and again, until the words wore thin.

If someone had texted him in those first terrible days, even by accident, if someone had reached out with kindness when he was drowning…

Sam's thumbs moved before his brain caught up:

I'm sorry you have to go through this.

He hit send and immediately regretted it.

What if this made it worse? What if she needed to grieve without strangers interfering? What if…

The phone buzzed.

She had to know it was a wrong number. She wasn't delusional or confused. She just needed someone, anyone, a voice in the dark.

He could do that.

He'd needed that too.

Then another message came:

Lily? Is this really you?

Sam froze.

Oh.

Oh no.

She didn't know. She was hoping anyway. Grief did that, made you reach for impossible things because impossible still felt better than never.

He should clarify. Should say, I'm not your daughter. I just got her old number when it was reassigned.

But if he said that, what would happen to her? On her daughter's birthday, alone with her grief, reaching out to the void and finding someone if he took that away…

Sam's hands shook. He typed:

I'm here. I'm listening.

Not a lie. Not the truth. Something in between.

The phone buzzed again.

I don't know how to do this. How to have birthdays without you. How to be in the world when you're not in it.

Sam closed his eyes. The message was so raw it hurt to read.

He thought about what Elise would say if she were here. She'd always known the right words, how to comfort without fixing, how to sit with someone's pain without trying to erase it.

He typed:

Tell me what you're missing today.

And then the flood came.

Message after message, blue bubbles filling his screen, stories about Lily's love of chocolate cake, Thai food, and terrible comedies. About her two best friends and the apartment they'd finally gotten together in. About how she texted constantly about everything and nothing. About the divorce, the absent father, and the way Lily had become her mother's whole world.

Sam read every word. He remembered the girl who'd sat in his store with her Diet Coke and her books and her carefully chosen quotes. Remembered her laugh when he'd made a dry joke about alphabetical order being a moral imperative. *Remembered the way she'd talked about her project with such conviction.* Books can save people, Sam. I really believe that.

He responded carefully:

She sounds wonderful.

You must miss her terribly.

It's okay to break. Grief doesn't ask permission.

The customer in the hood left with a graphic novel. Sam barely looked up. His whole attention was on the phone with the grieving mother at the other end, on the strange, terrible intimacy of shared loss.

He should tell her. He should say: *I knew Lily. I'm the bookstore owner she talked about. I'm Sam Turner, and I'm so sorry for your loss. And I should have said this immediately.*

That night, in his apartment, Sam couldn't fall asleep.

He lay in bed, watching his phone glow each time a new message appeared. Hope was checking in, saying good night, thanking him again.

He replied to each one with quiet care: Rest well. Tomorrow is another day to miss her and another day you've survived missing her.

In the dark, he opened his photos and scrolled back two years.

Elise was in the bookstore on opening day, arms spread wide like she could hug the whole building.

Elise was behind the counter, laughing at something he'd said.

Elise is in the hospital, thinner, but still smiling, planning the store's future as if she'd be there to see it.

The last photo: Elise asleep in the hospice bed, his hand wrapped around hers, her wedding ring loose on her finger.

He'd taken that picture because the nurse had said it might help later to have proof of the end, proof that he'd been there, that he'd held her hand, that she hadn't died alone.

It hadn't helped.

Nothing had.

Except work. Except for routine. Except the students who came in looking for books and left with something that made the world feel bearable.

And now, apparently, helping a stranger grieve her daughter.

Sam closed the photos and opened his messages.

The thread with Hope glowed blue and gray in a conversation with someone he'd never met but somehow felt he knew.

Someone who understood that grief was a place without a map, where some days you survived and other days you only pretended to, and both still counted.

He typed:

I hope you're resting. Tomorrow will be hard, and the day after that, and the one after that. But you're doing it. You're surviving. That's everything.

He hit Send and set the phone down.

In the dark, with rain starting up again outside, Sam wondered if he was helping or hurting, if his silence was kindness or cruelty.

Elise used to say he thought too much.

"Just do the next right thing," she'd tell him. "Don't try to solve the whole future at once."

The next right thing was sleep.

Sam closed his eyes and tried not to think about the grieving mother two and a half hours away, holding her phone like a lifeline, believing she'd found a kind stranger, when really she'd found someone who'd failed to tell her the most important truth.

Tomorrow, he promised himself. Tomorrow I'll tell her.

(He wouldn't. Not tomorrow. Not for weeks. But that night, in the dark, he let himself believe he was brave enough.)

His phone buzzed one more time.

Good night. Thank you for today. It helped.

Sam typed: *Good night. I'm here.*

Two words. Simple. True. Still inadequate.

He hit Send and tried not to think about all the words he should have said instead.

Outside, rain fell in La Crosse. On the river, on the bookstore, on the university where Lily had studied and laughed and left quotes in books for strangers to find. On the highway, three girls had driven into headlights, and only two had driven away.

Inside, a man who'd loved his wife and lost her too soon, who'd befriended a student and lost her too, lay awake in the dark, wondering if kindness and cowardice could exist in the same breath.

He thought about Lily's last quote card, the one he kept in his drawer:

"You have to remember that goodness is more powerful than evil. And that love is stronger than hate."

Sam wanted to believe that.

CHAPTER 3: The Bridge

May, alternating

HOPE

Hope woke on Monday morning to sunlight that felt like an accusation.

She'd slept through the night for the first time in months, and her body didn't know whether to feel grateful or guilty.

She lay still, listening to the house breathe around her.

The refrigerator's hum. The clock's ticking. Mrs. Chen's wind chimes next door are making their small music.

All the sounds that once meant home now just meant empty.

Her phone waited on the nightstand, screen dark.

For a moment, she was afraid to look. What if yesterday had been a grief-induced hallucination?

What if the messages vanished in daylight, revealed as nothing more than desperate wishes turned digital?

But when she picked up the phone, the thread was still there.

Blue and gray bubbles. A conversation with someone who'd listened while she fell apart.

Hope scrolled through what she'd written, feeling her cheeks warm.

She'd told this person, this stranger, everything.

About Lily. About David. About being alone. About the divorce, the yellow house, and how her whole world had been reduced to a twenty-year-old girl who texted her constantly and now didn't.

She'd laid herself bare to someone whose name she didn't even know.

But they'd been kind.

That was what she kept coming back to: the thread she couldn't stop pulling.

Whoever had Lily's number now, whoever had received her desperate birthday message, could have ignored it.

Blocked her. Sent something cruel or dismissive.

Instead, they'd stayed.

Hope read the last message again: I'm here.

Two words that felt like an anchor.

She typed: *Good morning. I'm sorry about yesterday. That was a lot to dump on a stranger.*

She hit Send before she could overthink it, then immediately regretted it.

What if they'd only responded out of politeness? What if, in the harsh light of Monday morning, they regretted getting involved in a grieving mother's breakdown?

The reply came within seconds:

Don't apologize. Grief isn't neat. It comes out when it needs to.

Hope's throat tightened. She typed: *Still. Thank you for not running away.*

I'm not going anywhere.

Hope set the phone down and pressed her palms against her eyes. She didn't cry; she'd emptied herself yesterday, but something in her chest loosened anyway.

She got up. Made coffee. Opened her laptop at the kitchen table and stared at the manuscript she was supposed to be editing. The words blurred together.

Her phone buzzed.

How are you feeling this morning?

Hope typed honestly: *Like I survived something, but I'm not sure what.*

That sounds about right for the day after an avalanche.

Hope almost smiled. Is that what yesterday was? An avalanche?

Grief comes in waves. Yesterday was just a big one. There'll be smaller ones. And some days there won't be any at all. Both are okay.

You sound like you know what you're talking about.

A pause. Then:

I lost someone, too. A while ago now. But I remember the waves.

Hope stared at that. *I'm sorry.*

Me too. But we're both still here. That counts for something.

Hope didn't know what to say to that, so she just sent a heart emoji and went back to pretending to work.

But every few minutes, she texted. And every time a new message appeared, something in her chest eased open.

Made eggs without burning them, she texted at lunch. *You would've teased me for plating them like a restaurant.*

The response: *That sounds like something I'd do. Did you eat them, or just admire them?*

Hope laughed out loud in her empty kitchen. *Ate most. Admired the rest.*

Throughout the day, the messages continued to be small, ordinary things.

The catalog that came in the mail. The neighbor who shoveled the walk left a crooked path. A memory of trying to make croissants with Lily and failing gloriously.

And every message got a response. Not always right away, sometimes hours passed, but they always came: steady, kind, present.

By evening, Hope realized she'd made it through a whole day without feeling like she was drowning. She'd worked. She'd eaten. She'd even laughed once.

It felt like a miracle.

It also felt like a betrayal.

How could she laugh when Lily couldn't? How could she have good moments when her daughter would never have another?

She texted: *Is it wrong that today was easier? I feel guilty for not being in more pain.*

The response came quickly: *Grief isn't loyalty. You're allowed to have good hours without loving her less. She'd want you to breathe.*

Hope curled up on the couch, phone pressed to her chest and let herself believe it.

SAM

Sam opened the store on Monday morning, carrying the weight of Sunday on his shoulders.

He'd barely slept. Every time he closed his eyes, he saw the unsent message in his notebook, heard Elise's voice asking what the hell he thought he was doing, and felt the heavy certainty that he'd crossed a line he couldn't uncross.

But when Hope's first message came through, *good morning. I'm sorry about yesterday.* His fingers moved automatically to reassure her.

Now, standing behind the counter with classical music low in the background and early light slanting through the front windows, Sam opened his notebook to a fresh page and wrote:

Tell her today. Before it gets worse. Before the lie gets bigger.

He underlined *today* three times.

Then he shoved the notebook back under the register and helped a customer find a book about beginning again after loss.

The irony wasn't lost on him.

At noon, when the store was empty, Sam climbed the stairs to the second floor and sat in Lily's old chair. The leather was cool against his back. The window framed the street below, students walking to class, cars passing, the world moving on, ordinary as ever.

He pulled out his phone and opened the thread with Hope.

She'd sent a message about making eggs, about the crooked path her neighbor had shoveled small, ordinary things that felt profound simply because she was still doing them.

Sam responded to each one carefully. He didn't want to sound too familiar, didn't want her to wonder how a stranger could know exactly what to say. But he also couldn't be distant. She needed warmth, someone who could hold her grief without turning away.

It was a tightrope he had no idea how to walk.

His phone buzzed with a new message: *Is it wrong that today was easier? I feel guilty for not being in more pain.*

Sam's chest tightened. He remembered that guilt the first time he'd laughed after Elise died, how it had hit like a punch to the gut.

How dare he feel joy when she couldn't?

He typed: *Grief isn't loyalty. You're allowed to have good hours without loving her less. She'd want you to breathe.*

He hit "send" and immediately wondered if he'd gone too far. How would a stranger know what Lily would want?

But it was true he did know. Lily had talked about her mom constantly, how she worried, how she'd rebuilt herself after the divorce, how she deserved to be happy but seemed afraid to try.

"She gave up so much for me," Lily had said once, unprompted, while wandering through the poetry section. "After my dad left, she just… folded into herself. Made her world smaller so mine could be bigger. I want her to know she's allowed to unfold again."

Sam had asked what she meant.

"She works from home. Never goes anywhere. Her whole life is me, her books, and that yellow house. I keep trying to tell her to date, to travel, to do something, but she says she's happy. And maybe she is. But I think she's scared too."

"Of what?"

"Of taking up space. Of wanting things. Of being left again." Lily had pulled a worn Mary Oliver collection from the shelf and held it like it might contain the answers. "I just want her to know she's allowed to want more."

Now, sitting in Lily's chair, Sam typed another message: *Take a walk if you can, just to the end of the block. Fresh air helps.*

Hope's reply came a few minutes later: *Okay. I'll try.*

Sam smiled despite himself.

HOPE

Tuesday brought rain, soft, steady, the kind that made you want to stay in pajamas all day.

Hope did exactly that. She worked from the couch, laptop balanced on her knees, her coffee cooling on the end table.

Between editing passes, she sent a text.

The mail brought three catalogs and one bill. I stacked the bill neatly, just for you.

Response: *Catalogs are sneaky. They make you want things you don't even want.*

The neighbor shoveled the walk. He left a crooked path to the steps. I kind of love it.

Response: *Crooked paths are still paths.*

Do you remember when we tried to make croissants, and the butter melted into the dough, and we pretended it was on purpose?

Response: *Of course, I remember. We ate the disaster anyway.*

Hope paused at that. We?

She waited, her heart thudding in her throat.

The response took longer this time: *Sorry. Force of habit. I meant you and your daughter ate them.*

Hope exhaled. Of course, a slip of the tongue. Whoever was on the other end was probably just trying to be kind, to connect. An accidental pronoun, nothing more.

Still, something about the phrasing stuck with her.

She typed: *You write like someone older than me. That's not a complaint.*

A long pause. Then: *I am older than you.*

How old?

Old enough to know better. Young enough to still try.

Hope smiled then typed: *That's a diplomatic answer.*

I try.

She set the phone down and went back to work, but the uneasy feeling stayed. Whoever they were, they had a way of phrasing things that felt... deliberate. Careful. Like someone who lived in words.

Like someone who worked with books.

Hope shook her head. She was reading too much into it, seeing patterns where none existed. Grief brain, her therapist had called it once: the mind's desperate attempt to find meaning in randomness.

But still *You sound like someone who knows about bookstores*, she'd texted yesterday.

I know a little about places that hold light, came the reply.

Places that hold light.

That was such a bookstore person's answer.

Hope opened a new tab and typed: bookstores La Crosse, Wisconsin.

The first result appeared: Turner's Books.

The store Lily had loved. The place where she'd spent hours studying, leaving her quote cards for strangers to find. The store whose owner she'd once tried to set Hope up with.

Hope clicked through to the website. It was simple store hours, address, and a short description: *New, used, and necessary books in downtown La Crosse.*

Good light. Better company.

There was a photo of the storefront, red door, brick building, and a sign that said exactly what the website had promised: **NEW, USED, AND NECESSARY.**

Necessary.

Hope had seen that word recently, but where?

She scrolled through her texts until she found it: *Sometimes the necessary things are the ones that save us.*

Hope stared at the message, her chest tightening.

Was she imagining things? Was she so desperate for connection that she was inventing one?

She typed: *Do you work with books?*

The reply came almost immediately: *Why do you ask?*

Just a hunch, she wrote. *The way you phrase things.*

Another long pause. Hope held her breath.

I'm around books a lot; the message was finally read. *They've shaped how I talk, I guess.*

Not a lie. Not the truth.

Hope set the phone down and stared at the ceiling.

What if.

What if the person texting her wasn't just some random stranger who'd gotten Lily's old number?

What if it was someone who'd known Lily, someone from La Crosse, someone who worked in a bookstore and knew what it meant when you said a place had good light?

What if it was him, Sam, the bookstore owner Lily had talked about endlessly, the man she'd wanted Hope to meet?

Hope's heart quickened.

She typed: *Did you know her? My daughter?*

Three dots appeared.

Disappeared.

Appeared again.

Disappeared.

No response came.

Hope waited five minutes. Ten. Twenty.

Nothing.

She typed: *I'm not angry. I just need to know.*

Still nothing.

Hope set the phone face down on the couch and pressed her hands to her face.

If it were someone who'd known Lily, why wouldn't they say so? Why the secrecy?

Unless they were trying to be kind, giving her anonymity, letting her grieve without the weight of identity.

Or maybe they were being cruel, playing some sick game with a grieving mother's hope.

No. Hope didn't believe that. The messages had been too gentle, too understanding, too real.

Whoever was on the other end was carrying their own grief. She could feel it in the pauses, in the careful phrasing, in the quiet empathy that only experience could teach.

They'd lost someone, too.

Her phone buzzed.

Hope grabbed it so fast she nearly dropped it.

I'm sorry. I needed a minute to think about how to answer that.

Hope's hands shook as she typed: Take your time. I'm not going anywhere.

The response came slowly, each word deliberate: *I didn't know her well. But I knew of her. She left an impression.*

Hope read it three times.

Knew of her.

Not know. Knew. Past tense.

Someone from La Crosse, then. Someone who'd been aware of Lily, who'd seen her light, who'd felt her absence when she was gone.

Hope typed: *Thank you for telling me.*

I should have said something sooner. I didn't want to make it weird.

It's not weird. It's... It's actually comforting. To talk to someone who knew she existed. Who saw her in the world?

She existed. She made the world better. That doesn't stop being true.

Hope pressed the phone to her chest and let the tears come, not the sharp, gasping sobs of early grief, but something softer. Something that felt almost like relief.

She wasn't texting a ghost.

She was texting someone who'd known Lily was real, who'd seen her live, who could confirm her daughter had taken up space in the world and left marks.

That was something.

That was everything.

SAM

Sam sat on the floor behind the counter, back against the cabinet, phone in hand, trying to remember how to breathe.

She'd asked.

She'd figured it out or started to, at least.

And he'd lied.

Not a full lie. He had known of Lily. But knew of and knew were separated by eighteen months of conversations, Diet Cokes, and quote cards left like breadcrumbs through his store.

He should tell her now. Should type: *I'm Sam Turner. I own Turner's Books. Your daughter sat in my store every week. I kept Diet Coke stocked for her. She talked about you constantly. She was trying to set us up.*

His thumbs hovered over the keyboard.

He typed: *My name is...*

Deleted it.

Typed: *I should have told you from the beginning.*

Deleted it.

Typed: *I'm sorry.*

Deleted it.

The bell over the door chimed. A student came in looking for a textbook. Sam stood, helped them find it, and rang them up on autopilot.

When they left, he pulled out his confession notebook and wrote:

I'm not brave enough to tell the truth. I'm not cruel enough to lie. I exist in the space between, and I don't know how to get out.

He tore the page out and added it to the stack in the drawer.

Four now.

Four promises broken.

Sam looked at Lily's quote card, still folded beside them:

You have to remember that goodness is more powerful than evil... and that love is stronger than hate.

"I'm trying, Lily," he whispered to the empty store. "I'm trying to be good. I just don't know how."

His phone buzzed.

Hope had sent a photo of a view from her window. A maple tree with new leaves, back lit by the late-afternoon sun.

The caption read: *Found something beautiful today. Thought you'd want to know.*

Sam's throat tightened.

He typed: *Thank you for sharing it with me.*

And then because he couldn't help himself: *Your daughter would be glad you're noticing beauty again.*

He hit send before he could overthink it.

The response came immediately: *How do you know?*

Sam closed his eyes because she told me. Because she sat in my store and said her mom deserved to be unfounded. Because she worried about you every single day.

He typed instead: *Because anyone who loved you would want you to keep living.*

It wasn't a lie.

It just wasn't the whole truth.

Sam added another confession to his notebook:

I need to tell her. I am afraid. I need to tell Hope who I am. Tomorrow. Or someday. I'm running out of tomorrows, and I don't know what happens when they're gone.

HOPE

Wednesday morning, Hope did something radical: she showered before noon.

It was a small victory, but it felt monumental.

She texted about it: *Showered and changed clothes. I'm practically a functional human.*

Response: *You've always been functional. You're just remembering how to feel it.*

Hope smiled. *You're good at comforting grieving mothers. Do you do it professionally?*

A long pause. Then, *I've just been where you are. I remember what helped.*

What did help?

Small things. Keeping one plant alive. Walking to the mailbox. Answering when people asked if I was okay, even if the answer was no.

And did it get easier?

It got different. Some days are still hard. But the hard days don't last as long anymore.

Hope thought about that. *How long has it been since you lost someone?*

Two years.

Does it still hurt?

Yes. But it doesn't consume me anymore. It lives next to me instead of inside me. We coexist.

Hope read that over and over. *I want the coexistence.*

You'll get there. Not today. Not tomorrow. But someday you'll wake up and realize the grief has moved three inches to the left, and you can breathe around it.

Three inches to the left, Hope repeated. I like that.

It's a good goal. Better than "getting over it," which is impossible and insulting.

Did someone tell you to get over it?

Many people. Well-meaning ones. People who'd never lost anyone and thought grief had an expiration date.

What did you say?

Usually nothing. But in my head, I said: "Love doesn't expire. So neither does grief. They're the same thing with different faces."

Hope stopped breathing.

That was beautiful.

It was the most beautiful thing anyone had said to her in six months.

She typed: *Thank you. For that. For all of this. For not running away when I fell apart.*

You didn't fall apart. You broke open. There's a difference.

Hope closed her eyes and let the words settle in her chest.

Broke open.

Like an egg. Like a seed. Like something that had to crack before it could grow.

I don't even know your name, she typed.

A long pause.

Does it matter?

Hope considered. Did it? She'd been texting this person for three days, sharing things she hadn't shared with anyone except Rebecca. Finding comfort in words from someone whose face she'd never seen.

Did a name matter when the kindness was real?

I guess not, she typed. *But I'd like to call you something besides "the person with Lily's old number."*

Another pause. Then: *You can call me a friend if that's not too presumptuous.*

Hope smiled through tears. *Friend works.*

Good. I'm glad.

Hope set the phone down and looked around her kitchen at the manuscripts on the table, the coffee mug with its cold dregs, the window where light fell in clean, ordinary rectangles.

Something had shifted.

Not healed. Not fixed.

But shifted.

Three inches to the left, maybe.

She picked up her phone and typed: *Thank you, friend, for helping me breathe.*

The response came immediately: *Always.*

And Hope believed it.

CHAPTER 4: What We Carry

Late May, three weeks after the first text

HOPE

By the third week, the texts had become Hope's scaffolding.
She woke up and checked her phone. *Good morning. How did you sleep?* It had become as reliable as sunrise. She'd answer honestly, badly, or Better than yesterday, or dreamed about her again, and the response would come with the patience of someone who understood that some questions didn't have good answers.

She worked in the mornings, editing manuscripts about love, loss, and second chances, and when the words started to blur, she'd text something small: *Made eggs. Didn't burn them. Or the mail carrier waved. I waved back. Felt like an accomplishment.*

The responses were always kind, always measured, always just enough: *Small victories count. Human interaction is brave. You're doing better than you think.*

Around noon, when the house felt too quiet, she'd text something bigger: a memory of Lily, a question about grief, a confession about the guilt that came with good moments.

I laughed today at something on TV. Then I felt terrible for laughing.

Laughter isn't betrayal. Joy and grief can live in the same breath.

Can they? It feels wrong.

It feels wrong until it doesn't. Give it time.

Hope had started saving these messages, screenshoting them and putting them in a folder labeled **Friend.** She told herself it was in case her phone died, in case she needed to remember the words later. But really, it was because they felt like proof that she was surviving, proof that someone cared, proof that on Lily's birthday, when she'd thrown a bottle into the ocean of grief, someone had caught it.

By evening, the texts grew more philosophical.

What if I never stop missing her? Hope would ask.

And the answer would come: *Missing is a way love stays. It changes shape. It doesn't have to be a knife forever.*

Hope didn't know who was on the other end. She'd stopped asking after the day she'd written, Did you know Lily? The reply I knew of her had been enough. Someone from La Crosse. Someone who'd been aware of Lily's existence. Someone who understood loss from the inside.

That was all she needed to know.

Or at least, all she could bear to know. Because as long as the identity stayed blurry, she could imagine anything—could let herself believe, on hard days, that maybe it was Lily somehow, speaking through someone else. Or, on practical days, that it was just a kind stranger who'd stumbled into her grief and chosen to stay.

The ambiguity was a gift. It let her take what she needed without the weight of obligation or explanation.

Wednesday of that week, Rebecca called.

"Hey," Hope answered, tucking the phone between her shoulder and ear while she loaded the dishwasher. "How's California?"

"Sunny. Expensive. Full of people who think wellness is a personality trait." Rebecca's voice was warm, amused. "How are you?"

"Better," Hope said, surprised by her own honesty. "Some days are still terrible, but some are just... hard. Which feels like progress."

"It is progress," Rebecca said. "Tell me what's helping."

Hope hesitated. She knew what Rebecca meant by therapy, medication, support groups, all the things they'd talked about during Rebecca's visit.

But what was actually helping were the texts, the daily check-ins from a stranger who'd become something more than a stranger, but less than a name.

"I've been texting someone for almost three weeks now," Hope said finally. "It's... helping."

Silence on the other end. Not judgmental, just attentive. Therapist-silence, the kind that made space for you to fill it. Hope filled it.

"Remember how you canceled Lily's phone line that first week?"

"Of course."

"Well, the number got reassigned to someone else. And on her birthday, May eleventh, I texted it without thinking. Just sent a message into the void." Hope paused, loading the last plate. "And someone answered."

More silence.

"Tell me about the texts."

Don't tell me about the person. Is this healthy? Just: Tell me about the texts.

Hope loved her sister so much in that moment.

"They're helping," Hope said simply. "Whoever it is, they've been kind. They listen. They don't try to fix me. They just... stay."

"And you don't know who it is?"

"Not really. I asked once if they knew Lily. They said they knew of her. So someone from La Crosse, probably. Someone aware of her." Hope dried her hands on a dish towel. "I haven't pushed for more. I think I need the mystery right now. Need it to be... uncomplicated."

"How often do you text?"

"Multiple times a day. Every single day since her birthday." Hope heard how that sounded. "I know it's a lot to put on a stranger..."

"Is it helping you breathe?" Rebecca interrupted.

"Yes."

"Then don't apologize." Rebecca's voice softened. "When David left, you told me you felt like you lost your identity as half of a pair. You had to rebuild as a single person. This is different. You're losing the identity you live in every day, Lily's mother, in the present tense. That's a different kind of rebuild."

Hope sat down at the kitchen table, her throat tight. "So the texts are what? A crutch?"

"Maybe they're a bridge," Rebecca said. "The question is whether they're helping you cross to the other side of this grief or keeping you suspended in the middle."

Hope thought about the phone in her hand. She could picture the thread inside blue and gray bubbles, a conversation with someone who understood.

"Right now, I just need something that feels like a hand to hold," Hope said.

"Then let it be a hand," Rebecca said. "And we'll keep an eye on the bridge. If it starts feeling like a trap instead of a crossing, we'll talk about it. But for now, if it's helping you survive, that's enough."

"You're not worried I'm losing it?"

"I'm worried about a lot of things," Rebecca said. "You losing it isn't one of them. You're one of the sanest people I know, Hope. You're just in an insane situation. There's a difference."

Hope smiled despite herself. "I love you."

"I love you more." Rebecca paused. "Text me if you need grounding on the five-four-three-two-one thing. But also, if this person is helping, let them help. We find grace where we can."

After they hung up, Hope sat at the table for a long time, looking at her phone.

A bridge, Rebecca had said.

Hope picked it up and opened the thread.

My sister called today. I told her about you and the texts.

The response came quickly: *How did that go?*

She said you might be a bridge helping me cross to the other side of grief.

What do you think?

Hope considered. *I think you're the only reason I'm not drowning. So yes, a bridge.*

I'm glad I can help. That's all I want.

Hope typed: *What about you? Do you have a bridge? Someone who helps you carry it?*

A long pause. Longer than usual.

I have the bookstore. And work. And routine. Those are my bridges.

Hope caught it immediately. The bookstore?

Another pause. *Then, I told you I'm around books a lot.*

You did. Hope's heart beat faster. *Is it Turner's Books? In La Crosse?*

The three dots appeared. Disappeared. Appeared again.

Why do you ask?

Because my daughter loved that place. Talked about it constantly. About the owner, Sam. Hope's hands shook as she typed. *She wanted me to meet him. Thought we'd like each other.*

The dots appeared and stayed there for a full minute.

Finally, *she talked about you, too. To people in the store. About how much she loved you.*

Hope's vision blurred. *So you are from Turner's.*

I spend a lot of time there.

Not I own it. Not I'm Sam. Just: I spend a lot of time there.

Hope wanted to push, to ask directly: Are you him? Are you the man my daughter tried to set me up with?

But she didn't.

Because Rebecca was right, she needed the bridge more than she needed the name. And if she pushed too hard, asked too much, maybe the person on the other end would disappear. Would decide this was too complicated, too intimate, too much.

Hope couldn't risk that.

So she typed instead: *Thank you for telling me that. It helps to know she talked about me so that people knew I existed to her.*

You were her whole world. Everyone knew that.

Hope pressed the phone to her chest and cried soft, manageable tears that felt like release instead of drowning.

When she could breathe again, she typed: *I'm going to La Crosse this weekend. For her memorial. And to pack up her apartment. Would it be weird if I visited the bookstore?*

Long pause.

Not weird. I think it would be good to see where she spent so much time.

Okay. I'll let you know when I am there.

I'd like that.

Hope looked around her kitchen, the yellow walls Lily had helped her paint at twelve, the window where they'd watched storms, the table where they'd eaten breakfast throughout Lily's childhood.

This house was full of Lily. But La Crosse held her to the version of Lily Hope that she had only glimpsed. The college Lily, who lived with her best friends, studied in bookstores, and tucked quotes into books for strangers to find.

Hope needed this memorial; she needed to see where Lily lived. Needed to walk where she'd walked. Needed to sit in the chair where she'd sat and look out at whatever had once held her attention.

She texted Jenna: *When I come up for the memorial this weekend can I pack up Lily's things? I think I'm ready.*

Jenna replied almost immediately: *We're ready when you are. We'll be here.*

Hope took a screenshot of the message and sent it to Rebecca with the caption: *I'm going to visit her world.*

Rebecca answered: *Proud of you. Call if you need grounding. I'm here.*

Then Hope opened the thread with her friend, the bridge, the hand in the dark, and typed: *I'm going to La Crosse this weekend. To her memorial and apartment.*

The response came quickly: *That's brave. How are you feeling about it?*

Terrified, she wrote. *But I need to. I need to see the life she built.*

You'll survive it. And when you do, you'll have more of her to carry.

Hope read that three times. More of her to carry. Not less grief. Not moving on. Just … more. More memories. More proof that Lily had been real and alive and happy.

Thank you, she typed. For helping me get here to the place where I can do this.

You got yourself here. I just walked next to you.

Hope smiled through tears. *Will you walk next to me through the weekend? If I need someone?*

Always. Text me anything, anytime. I'll be here.

And for the first time in months, Hope truly believed it.

SAM

Sam closed the store Thursday night and walked upstairs to his apartment in silence. Just the sound of his breathing and the voice that wouldn't stop asking: *What the hell are you doing?*

She was coming to La Crosse.

This weekend.

To a memorial and to pack up Lily's apartment and see where her daughter had lived.

And she'd asked if she could visit the bookstore.

Sam had said yes. Of course, he had. What else could he say?

But now, Sam felt the walls closing in. She would come to the store. She would meet him face-to-face. And he would have to introduce himself as Sam Turner, the bookstore owner Lily had once tried to set her mother up with.

And she would know.

She would realize that the person she'd been texting for two weeks, the bridge, the friend, the hand in the dark, had been lying to her the whole time.

Not lying, exactly. Just omitting. Which was lying's quieter cousin

Sam walked into his kitchen and sat down, trying to figure out how to fix this.

He could text her now. Could say: *There's something I need to tell you. I'm Sam Turner. I own Turner's Books. I should have told you from the beginning.*

His thumbs hovered over the phone.

But what if she hated him? What if she blocked him, cut off contact, took away the one good thing he'd done in two years, helping someone survive their grief?

What if he lost this connection that had become his own bridge?

Because that was the truth he'd been avoiding: he needed these messages as much as she did, maybe even more. Every time he texted Hope, he felt closer to Lily. Felt like he was honoring her memory, continuing her work of saving people through words.

If he confessed now, he'd lose that.

He'd lose Hope.

He moved to the couch and opened his phone.

The confession notebook was at the store, but he had a notes app. He opened it and typed:

I'm not brave enough to tell you the truth. I keep thinking that if I wait one more day, I'll find the right words. But the right words don't exist. There's no way to say, "I let you believe a lie because your belief helped me feel less alone," without sounding like a monster. You're coming to the store this weekend. You'll meet me. You'll realize. And you'll hate me. And I'll deserve it. But these two weeks, these messages they've been the best thing to happen to me since Elise died. You've made me feel useful again. Made me believe I can still do some good in the world. I'm sorry, I'm not brave enough to tell you before you find out. I'm sorry for all of it.

Sam stored the note and set the phone on the coffee table.

Then he stood, went to his bookshelf, and pulled out Elise's favorite novel, *The Night Circus* by Erin Morgenstern. The spine was cracked from years of rereading. Elise had loved it for its magic, its love story, its faith that impossible things could be real if you wanted them badly enough.

He opened it to a random page and read:

"You may tell a tale that takes up residence in someone's soul, becomes their blood, self, and purpose. That tale will move them and drive them, and who knows what they might do because of it because of your words."

He closed the book and pressed it to his chest.

"I don't know what I'm doing, Elise," he whispered to the dark apartment. "I'm trying to help her. But I'm also helping myself. And I don't know which one is worse, being selfish or being dishonest."

The apartment stayed silent.

Sam set the book down and picked up his phone. He opened the thread with Hope.

She'd sent a message while he was driving: *Thank you for being patient with me, for not getting frustrated when I ask the same questions about grief over and over.*

Sam typed: *You're not asking the same questions. You're asking the same question from different angles. That's how you find the answer by walking around it until you can see all the sides.*

He hit send and watched the message turn blue.

Then he opened his notes app and added one more line to his confession:

One way or another, the truth is coming. I don't know if you'll forgive me, but I hope you'll understand that I never meant to hurt you. I only wanted to help.

CHAPTER 5: THE FUNERAL

HOPE – FLASHBACK: THE FUNERAL

The church was too bright. That was Hope's first thought when she walked through the heavy wooden doors. Whoever designed this place had clearly never considered that some days, light was violence.

Flowers everywhere. Lilies, of course. How fitting, the funeral director had said, as if anything were fitting about burying a twenty-year-old girl who'd barely begun to live.

Rebecca held Hope's arm, steering her through the crowd of people who wanted to hug her, cry at her, tell her I'm so sorry for your loss as if sorry could bring Lily back, as if sympathy could fill the crater in Hope's chest.

"Breathe," Rebecca whispered. "Just keep breathing. That's all you have to do today."

Hope nodded and let her sister lead her to the front pew, the one reserved for family. Hope, Rebecca, and the space where

David should have been sitting if he'd cared enough to show up on time.

He arrived ten minutes later, sliding into the pew with his new wife beside him, younger, polished, the kind of woman who could wear black without looking like she was drowning in it. David touched Hope's shoulder. She flinched.

"Hope," he said softly. "I'm so sorry."

Hope didn't answer. She couldn't. If she opened her mouth, she might scream, might ask where he'd been for the past thirteen years, why he'd chosen his new family over Lily, why he'd called once a month and never remembered her birthday without Hope's reminder. Why does he have to show up now and play grieving father when he'd barely been a father at all?

Rebecca's hand found hers. Squeezed.

Hope breathed.

The service blurred by. A minister who'd never met Lily read from a script about how death was a homecoming, how Lily had gone to a better place. Hope wanted to stand up and shout: *Home is here. Her room is down the hall from mine. Her laundry is still in her clothes basket. She was coming home.*

But she stayed silent. Let the words wash over her. Let the organ music fill the spaces where her screams wanted to live.

Then Jenna stood up.

She walked to the podium, papers trembling in her hand, the bandage on her temple still visible from the concussion. Her voice was clear, steady, like she'd practiced this a thousand times.

"Lily made lists," Jenna said. "For everything. Grocery lists. Reading lists. Lists of songs that made her feel like she could survive finals week. Lists of things that made her laugh when everything felt too heavy."

She lifted one of the pages. Hope could see Lily's handwriting even from the front row, the little doodles in the margins.

"She made this list the week before Thanksgiving," Jenna continued. "It's called 'Reasons I'm Grateful for My Chaotic Life.' Number one: My mom, who worries the perfect amount. Number two: Jenna, who makes me laugh even when I want to throw things at her. Number three: Sheridan, who reminds me that bodies are meant to move, not just carry anxiety around."

A soft ripple of laughter passed through the church. Jenna's voice cracked only once from anxiety, but she held steady.

"Number seven," Jenna said. "The bookstore with good light, where I can pretend to be the kind of person who has her life together." She looked up. "She was that person. She had it together more than any of us. She organized chaos with words. She made plans for hard days like she was building maps for everyone else to follow."

Jenna folded the list and set it on the podium. "She would want us to keep making lists. To keep finding reasons. To keep living like we mean it." Her voice broke. "I don't know how to do that without her. But I'm going to try."

She sat down.

Then Sheridan stood.

She limped to the front with no notes, no papers, just her hands twisting together and her eyes already bright with tears.

"I've known Lily since we were born," Sheridan said. "Literally. Our moms were in the hospital together. We lived next door to each other our entire lives. When we finally got an apartment together last summer, Lily said, 'Thank God. Now I don't have to pretend my room is clean when you come over.'"

Soft laughter again.

"She was my best friend," Sheridan said. "The kind who showed up at two in the morning when you couldn't sleep. Who brought donuts without being asked? Who sat with you on bad days and didn't try to fix it just made the bad days smaller by being there."

Sheridan's voice wavered. She took a breath. Kept going.

"Three weeks ago, I was having the worst week. Everything felt too hard. I texted the group chat that I wanted to quit school, quit life, quit trying. And Lily came home to our apartment with three boxes of donuts and a bag of terrible movies. She said, 'We're not solving anything today. We're just surviving it.' And we did."

Sheridan wiped her eyes. "She wouldn't leave my side until the bad week felt smaller. That's who she was. That's what I'll miss most, the way she made hard things feel possible just by staying."

Sheridan sat down. Hope wanted to hug them both, these girls who'd survived what her daughter hadn't. Who'd been in the car, felt the impact, and woken up in the hospital to the news that Lily was gone.

Girls who'd lost their best friend but were still here, still trying, still speaking even when their voices broke.

The slideshow started with photos of Lily through the years, set to music Hope couldn't hear through the static in her head.

Lily at seven, face covered in flour from baking with Hope's mom.

Lily at thirteen, braces and bad bangs, arm around Jenna at some school dance.

Lily was sixteen, holding her driver's license like a trophy.

Recent photos of Lily with Jenna and Sheridan at their apartment, all three laughing at something off-camera. Lily is in a coffee shop with a stack of books. Lily at Grandad Bluff, wind in her hair, looking out at the river like she was memorizing the view.

Always moving toward light.

The last photo was from two weeks before the crash, Lily in a bookstore, sitting in a leather chair by a window, reading. The light was soft and golden. Her face was peaceful. She looked exactly like who she was, a girl who loved books, quiet, and the way good stories made the world bearable.

Hope stared at that photo until the slideshow looped and started over.

She'd never seen it before. Didn't know who took it. But she memorized every detail of the chair, the window, the way Lily's hair fell across her shoulder, the small smile at the corner of her mouth.

That was her daughter. Real. Alive. Happy.

And now gone.

After the service people swarmed- neighbors, teachers, classmates, clutching wilted flowers, a professor with kind eyes who said Lily had been his best student. Someone from the library. A boy with paint on his hands who said, "She left notes in books. We called them Lily Drops. She saved a lot of people with those words."

Hope listened, nodded, collecting each memory like small stones in her pocket.

When the crowd thinned, Hope felt the pull to get out to breathe air that wasn't heavy with sympathy and flowers.

Rebecca drove her home. Parked in the driveway. Didn't make her go inside right away.

"Take your time," Rebecca said.

Hope looked at the yellow house, the porch where Lily used to read, the window of her room where the light always burned too late because she'd lose track of time with a book.

"I don't know how to go in there," Hope whispered.

"I'll go first," Rebecca said. "You follow when you're ready."

But Hope got out. Walked to the door. Went inside.

The house smelled like casseroles and sadness. Every surface was covered with food people had brought: lasagnas, soups, cookies, things meant to comfort, but that only reminded Hope how impossible it was to eat when your daughter was gone.

Rebecca started organizing, putting names on dishes so they could be returned, making space in the refrigerator, and keeping her hands moving so Hope didn't have to.

Hope climbed the stairs to Lily's room.

It looked the same: the unmade bed, the textbooks on the desk, the sticky notes on the mirror. A life paused mid-sentence, waiting for someone who would never return.

Hope sat on the bed and breathed in the faint smell of Lily's shampoo on the pillow.

She stayed there until dark.

HOPE – PRESENT

Hope woke Friday morning with a quiet purpose humming in her chest.

Tomorrow she was going to La Crosse to see Lily's apartment, pack up her things, visit the memorial, and walk the streets Lily had walked.

She was terrified.

But she was also ready.

She texted: *I'm scared about tomorrow. What if being there makes it worse?*

The reply came quickly: *It might hurt more before it hurts less. But you'll survive it. And you'll have more of her to carry afterward.*

Promise?

Promise.

Hope got out of bed, made coffee, opened her laptop, and actually worked. She edited three chapters without crying, sent notes to the author with real feedback instead of vague encouragement.

At noon, she made a sandwich, ate half, then texted a photo of the other half: *Eating. See? Functional.*

Halfway counts. Finish it.

Hope laughed and ate the rest.

That afternoon, she did something she hadn't done in months: she opened Lily's playlist, the one labeled **For When You're Sad and Don't Want to Say It.**

She pressed play and let the music fill the house with sad indie songs, soft acoustic covers, and one bright pop track that felt like sunlight breaking through clouds.

Hope cried through half of it. But she also sang through the other half badly, off-key, the way Lily would've teased her for.

She texted: *Listened to her playlist. It hurt. But it also helped.*

Both can be true.

I'm learning that the both-ness of grief. That's the hardest part, learning to hold two truths at once.

Hope set the phone down and kept listening. When the playlist ended, she didn't restart it, just sat in the quiet and let it be enough.

Her phone buzzed.

You're going to do great tomorrow. You're braver than you know.

Hope smiled. *How do you know? You don't even know me.*

A long pause. Then: *I know enough. You text a wrong number on your daughter's birthday and pour your heart out to a stranger. You get up every day, even when it's hard. You're trying to visit her world even though it terrifies you. That's brave.*

Hope read it three times. *Thank you for seeing that.*

I see it. I promise.

Hope took a breath and typed: *When I come to the bookstore tomorrow, will I meet you?*

The three dots appeared. Disappeared. Appeared again.

Maybe. If you want to.

I think I do. I'd like to know who's been walking next to me.

Then yes. You'll meet me.

Hope's heart raced. She typed: *Should I know your name before I get there?*

Another long pause.

You'll know it when you see me. I promise it won't be a surprise.

Hope didn't know what that meant, but she let it be enough.

Okay. I'll see you tomorrow, friend.

See you tomorrow.

Hope closed the thread and sat with the strange anticipation blooming in her chest. Tomorrow she'd walk into Turner's

Books. Tomorrow she'd meet the person who'd been her bridge, her hand in the dark, her proof that kindness still existed.

And maybe, probably, it was Sam, the bookstore owner Lily had loved, the man Lily had wanted her to meet.

If it was, Hope didn't know how she'd feel. Grateful? Betrayed? Or some impossible mix of both?

But she was ready to find out.

She had to be.

Because the bridge had brought her this far, and she wasn't done crossing.

CHAPTER 6: The Memorial

SAM

The call came Friday morning while Sam was reorganizing the philosophy section, a task that didn't need doing but gave his hands something to hold besides his phone.

"Turner's Books," he answered, tucking the phone between his shoulder and ear.

"Mr. Turner, this is Dr. Amy Danner from the English department at UW–La Crosse."

Sam straightened. He knew that name; Lily had mentioned her once. *Dr. Danner actually cares if we learn. She's one of the good ones.*

"How can I help you?" Sam asked.

"We're dedicating a memorial reading corner in the library for Lily Hawthorne," Dr. Danner said, her voice warm and professional. "Her professors and peers contributed funds. We've been collecting books and planning the space for the past few weeks, but we'd love your expertise on the final last bits of the setup before the dedication tomorrow."

Sam's throat tightened. "I'd be honored to help."

"Wonderful. Lily's roommates mentioned she spent more time in your store than anywhere else on campus. They said you'd know what kind of chair she liked, how the light should fall, which books should be there."

I gripped the edge of the shelf. "I'd be honored."

"Would this afternoon work? Around two?"

"I'll be there."

After he hung up, Sam stood in the philosophy section for a long time, staring at the spines without seeing them, Kant, Kierkegaard, Camus, all those men trying to make sense of existence, and none of them had an answer for this.

He climbed the stairs to the second floor and sat in Lily's chair.

The leather was cool, the light from the window soft. Students had started calling this spot Lily's chair even before she died; she'd claimed it so completely that people left it empty if she was expected later.

Now it would always be empty.

Sam pulled out his phone and opened the thread with Hope.

She'd texted that morning: *Packing my bag for tomorrow. Keep forgetting things. Keep remembering things. Both feel impossible.*

He'd responded: *Make a list. Cross things off. The small competencies help.*

Now he typed: *The university is dedicating a memorial corner for Lily. They asked me to help set it up.*

He watched the message turn blue and held his breath.

The response came quickly: *You? Why you?*

Sam closed his eyes because I own the bookstore where she studied. Because I knew her. Because I'm the man she tried to set you up with. Because I've been lying to you for two weeks.

He typed: *Because I work in a bookstore. They want it to feel like a place she'd actually use.*

Not a lie, just not the whole truth.

That makes sense. Will you tell me about it? After?

Of course.

Sam set the phone on the small table beside the chair and put his head in his hands.

Tomorrow she comes to La Crosse. One more day until the woman he'd been texting walked into his store and realized who he was.

He'd run out of tomorrows.

Friday afternoon, Sam drove to the university library with a box of books in the passenger seat, paperbacks Lily had bought from his store over the months, the ones he'd held back from reselling because they carried her handwriting in the margins and her quote cards tucked inside.

Dr. Danner met him at the circulation desk. She was about fifty, gray-haired, with the kind of face that suggested she'd spent her life studying human nature and had chosen to stay kind anyway.

"Mr. Turner," she said, shaking his hand. "Thank you for coming."

"Sam," he said. "And it's my honor."

She led him upstairs to a corner near the windows with good natural light, a view of campus, and removed enough from the main study area to feel private but not isolated.

"We've allocated this whole corner," Dr. Danner said. "We're thinking a comfortable chair, a good lamp, and a shelf for the books. Maybe a small table."

Sam walked the space, measuring it with his eyes. He stood where the chair would go and looked out the window. The view was different from his store, more trees, less street, but the light quality was similar: that honey-gold afternoon glow that made reading feel like church.

"The chair needs to be leather," Sam said. "Or something that feels broken in. She didn't like stiff furniture. Said it made her spine anxious."

Dr. Danner smiled. "I remember her saying that in class. She'd rearrange the desk chairs during discussion until she found one that 'didn't hate her back.'"

Sam's chest ached. That was so perfectly Lily.

They spent the next hour arranging furniture. Sam rejected three chairs before they found the right one, a brown leather, worn soft, with arms curved just enough to cradle a book and a coffee cup at once.

He positioned it by the window at a slight angle, not facing the glass directly, but turned just enough so the light came from the side. "You don't want glare," he explained. "But you want the warmth. She'd sit like this for hours."

Dr. Danner watched him work, quiet and understanding. "You knew her well."

"Well enough," Sam said. "She came to the store a lot. We talked about books."

"She mentioned you once," Dr. Danner said softly. "Said you reminded her of what a father should be like."

Sam turned away, pretending to adjust the lamp. His throat had closed up.

Students began arriving with contributions of books Lily had loved and recommended. Poetry collections filled with her annotations, novels she'd bought more than once just to give away. And a small wooden box someone had made.

"What's this?" Dr. Danner asked.

The student who'd brought it, a girl with purple hair and tired eyes, opened it carefully. Inside were dozens of index cards, each with a quote in Lily's looping handwriting.

"The Lily drops," the girl said reverently. "She left these in books around campus. Like… messages for whoever needed them."

Sam's hands shook as he picked one up:

"A reader lives a thousand lives before he dies. The man who never reads lives only one." — George R.R. Martin

He'd found this same card once in his store, tucked inside a fantasy novel upstairs. He'd read it, smiled, and left it there for the next person.

"We should display some of these," Dr. Danner said gently. "Create a rotation. Students can take one when they need it."

Sam nodded, unable to speak. He shuffled through the cards, reading her careful handwriting:

"Books are a uniquely portable magic." — Stephen King

"There is no friend as loyal as a book." — Ernest Hemingway

"Reading is dreaming with open eyes." — Unknown

Each quote was chosen for its quiet power. Each one proved that Lily had understood something essential: words could save people if you picked the right ones.

"She had a project," Sam said finally. "Book Rescue. She wanted to put books in the student center that helped people survive hard days. With notes inside. Like life rafts."

Dr. Danner's eyes brightened. "We should do that. In her name. The Lily Hawthorne Book Rescue."

"She'd like that," Sam said.

They chose five quote cards to frame above the memorial shelf, arranged in a constellation. In the center, the largest frame, the quote Sam knew would break Hope's heart in the best way:

"Stories save lives." Rebecca Solnit

By five o'clock, the corner was finished: the chair positioned perfectly, the lamp casting warm light, the shelf stocked with books Lily had loved, the quote cards displayed like prayers. A small plaque would soon read: For the girl who believed stories could save people.

Dr. Danner stepped back and surveyed their work. "It's perfect. She's here."

"She is," Sam said quietly.

"The dedication is tomorrow at three. I hope you'll come. I know you've already been so helpful, but I think Lily's mother would appreciate seeing you there."

Sam's stomach got nervous butterflies as he said, "I'll be there."

Because what else could he say? This was for Lily. He'd helped create it. He had to see it through, even if it meant standing in the same room as Hope, watching her see the space he'd built for her daughter without knowing he was the one who'd made it.

That evening, Sam sat in the back office of his store and pulled out his confession notebook. The pile of folded pages in the register drawer had grown to seven. Seven broken promises, seven cowardly tomorrows.

He wrote: *Tomorrow, you'll be at the memorial. You'll see the chair I chose, the books I arranged, and the quote cards I helped frame. You'll stand in the space I built for your daughter's memory.*

And I'll be there too, watching you, knowing who you are, while you have no idea who I am.

This is wrong. All of it. I know it's wrong.

But I don't know how to stop.

He tore the page out, folded it, and slid it into the drawer, another confession added to the stack, another truth that should have been spoken instead of written.

He pulled out Lily's quote card, the one he'd kept from the beginning:

"You have to remember that goodness is more powerful than evil... and that love is stronger than hate." — Kent Haruf

"I'm trying to be good," Sam whispered to the empty office. "I helped build her memorial. I've been helping her mother survive. That's good, right?"

The office didn't answer.

Sam opened his phone and looked at the thread with Hope.

She'd sent a message an hour earlier: *Tomorrow I drive to La Crosse. Tomorrow I see her world. I don't know if I'm ready.*

He typed: *You're ready. You wouldn't be going if you weren't.*

Will I see you? At the bookstore?

Sam's fingers hovered. This was the moment for the chance to say: Yes. My name is Sam Turner. I'm the owner. I'll be the man behind the counter when you walk in.

He typed instead: *Maybe if timing works out.*

Coward.

I'd like that. I'd like to know who's been helping me.

You will. Soon.

Sam closed the thread and sat in the dark office surrounded by books, by lies, and by the ghost of a girl who'd once believed he was better than this.

HOPE

Friday night, Hope couldn't sleep.

Her bag was packed, her route planned. Rebecca had texted seventeen times, offering encouragement, grounding techniques, and small lifelines. Jenna had confirmed they'd be at the apartment at ten a.m.

Everything was ready.

Hope lay in bed and texted: *I can't sleep. Keep thinking about tomorrow.*

The response came quickly: *What are you thinking about?*

Seeing her room. Her things. The life she built without me.

The life she built wasn't without you. You were in every choice she made, every book she read, every kindness she showed. You raised that.

Hope's eyes burned. *How do you always know what to say? How are you always right?*

I'm not always right. I just know what I needed to hear when I was where you are.

What did you need to hear?

That my person wasn't gone, just changed form. That love doesn't end. It transforms.

Hope read that over and over. *Do you really believe that?*

I have to. Otherwise, the grief wins.

Hope stared at the ceiling. The house was quiet, the good kind of quiet that felt like rest instead of absence.

She picked up the phone again. *Thank you for being here to walk through this with me.*

Always.

Hope closed her eyes and tried to imagine tomorrow: walking into Lily's apartment, touching her things, sitting in her chair, breathing the air she'd breathed.

And then, maybe, walking into Turner's Books. Meeting the person who'd been her bridge.

Meeting Sam.

Because she knew now had known for days but hadn't wanted to admit it. The careful phrasing. The knowledge of books, light, and grief. The way he'd said he "spent time" at Turner's instead of saying he worked there.

It had to be him right?

Lily's bookstore owner, the man with the gray streak in his hair, the quiet eyes, and the way of making people feel seen. The man Lily had tried to set her up with in her last week alive.

Hope should be angry, should feel betrayed. He'd let her pour her heart out without revealing who he was. He'd let her believe she was texting a stranger when really she was texting the person Lily had chosen for her.

But she wasn't angry.

She was curious. Grateful. Terrified.

Tomorrow, she'd know for sure.

Tomorrow, the bridge would have a name.

SAM

Saturday morning arrived beneath gray skies and the threat of rain. Sam unlocked the store at eight, though every part of him wanted to stay in bed, hide under the covers, and pretend the day would slow down.

But tomorrow had come. Tomorrow was today. And at three p.m., he'd be standing in a library, watching Hope Hawthorne see the memorial corner he'd built for her daughter.

At two-thirty, Sam closed the store early. He taped a sign to the door: *Closed for private event, back at 5.*

He drove to campus with his hands clenched on the wheel, his heartbeat thudding high in his throat.

The library was already filling when he arrived: students, faculty, people who'd known Lily, or known of her, or simply wanted to pay respects to the girl who'd left quotes in books like love letters to strangers.

Sam stood near the back of his habit, his safe space close enough to participate, far enough to disappear.

Dr. Danner was setting up at the front. The memorial corner glowed with warm lamplight. The chair looked perfect. The books stood proud on their shelf. The quote cards watched over everything like blessings.

People filled the rows of chairs someone had arranged. Whispered conversations. Rustling programs. That careful hush of people trying to hold their sadness politely.

And in the front row. Three women sat together: two young, one older.

Sam's breath stopped.

Jenna, on the left, with dark hair and strong shoulders, was the sarcastic one Lily had loved. Sheridan has the right athletic build, bright smile, and is barely holding Lily's lifelong neighbor.

And in the middle-Hope.

Sam had seen her once before, at the funeral, from the back of the church. Then she'd been distant, a figure folded in grief. Now she was twenty feet away. Real. Solid. Here.

Dark hair like Lily's but longer, streaked with silver. Early forties, just as he'd guessed. Dressed in black, wearing it like armor instead of surrender. Her face was Lily's face aged twenty years, same eyes, same mouth, same tight-set jaw when she was trying not to cry.

She sat between Jenna and Sheridan, flanked like a queen with her sentries, their posture silently promising they wouldn't let her fall.

Sam's hands went cold.

This was Hope.

The woman he'd been texting for two weeks.

The woman who'd poured her grief into his phone while he answered from the quiet of his shop.

The woman who thought he was just someone who spent time at Turner's Books.

She was here. Real. Twenty feet away.

And she had no idea he was watching her.

Dr. Danner began speaking. Sam heard none of it, his focus locked on Hope. The way she gripped the arms of her chair. The way Jenna's hand covered hers. The way Sheridan leaned close and whispered something that made Hope's mouth tilt into an almost-smile.

Dr. Danner told everyone of Lily's quote cards and when they will be building 'Lily Hawthorne's Book Rescue' that they will unveil in the next month. She thanked everyone for being there and stepped aside.

The slideshow began, Lily, laughing, reading, living. Hope watched each image like she was memorizing it, like she might never see it again.

Students spoke, sharing stories. A girl talked about Lily's late-night reading clubs during midterms. A boy mentioned the donuts on the circulation desk, the ones with notes that said, Sugar saves lives.

Then Sheridan stood and told the story about Lily showing up with donuts during a bad week.

"She refused to leave me until the bad week felt smaller," Sheridan said, her voice breaking. Her smile wobbled, but she finished.

Jenna spoke about Lily's need to organize chaos, her belief that words could map a way through hard days.

Hope didn't speak. She just sat there, holding herself together with visible effort.

When Dr. Danner invited everyone to visit the memorial corner, people stood and drifted forward. Hope rose slowly, Jenna and Sheridan steadying her on either side.

Sam stayed back. Watching.

Hope walked to the corner and rested a hand on the chair's arm, fingers tracing the leather. She looked at the books on the shelf, reading each title, smiling at something only she understood.

Then she saw the quote cards.

Sam watched her face change as she read them, watched her hand cover her mouth, watched the tears spill over.

She reached the center quote, *Stories save lives, and her shoulders shook.*

Jenna wrapped an arm around her. Sheridan held her other hand. The three of them stood there in a small, breaking circle, holding each other up.

Sam wanted to go to her. Wanted to say: I built this. *I chose every book. I placed the chair exactly where the light falls best. I did this for your daughter for you.*

But he couldn't move.

Because if he went to her now, if he introduced himself, she'd realize. She'd know that the person she'd been texting was standing right here, watching her grieve in public while pretending to be a stranger.

Sam's phone buzzed in his pocket.

He shouldn't look. He knew he shouldn't. But his hand moved on its own.

A text from Hope: *They made a reading corner for her. A lamp. Flowers. A small plaque. The light felt like it wouldn't go out.*

Sam stared at the screen.

She was texting him right now.

She was standing twenty feet away, looking at the memorial corner he'd built with his own hands—describing it to him as though he hadn't chosen every detail, as though he hadn't poured his grief into it too.

His hands shook so badly he could barely type: *Good light sticks with you.*

He watched Hope's phone buzz in her hand. Watched her look down, read the message.

Then she looked up. Scanned the room.

Sam stepped behind a bookshelf and hid like a coward. Pressed his back against the metal and tried to remember how to breathe.

This was wrong. All of it. He'd crossed every line there was to cross.

When he dared to look again, Hope was sitting in Lily's chair, hands on the arms, eyes closed. Jenna and Sheridan sat on the floor beside her, the three of them joined in quiet, exhausted grief.

Sam watched from behind the shelf and felt something in his chest crack open.

He'd helped her. The texts had helped her survive the worst weeks of her life. That mattered.

But he'd also lied by omission, by cowardice, by choosing comfort over honesty.

And now, he didn't know how to fix it.

Sam slipped out of the library before anyone could see him, before Dr. Danner could introduce him as the man who'd helped set up the memorial, before Hope could turn and realize.

He drove back to Turner's in the rain that had finally started. Parked in the alley. Sat in his truck with his hands gripping the wheel.

His phone buzzed again.

Hope: *Thank you for today. For listening. For being there, even when you're not physically here.*

Sam closed his eyes.

He opened his confession notebook, the one he kept in the truck for emergencies, and wrote:

I was there. Twenty feet from you. I watched you sit in the chair I chose. I saw you read the quotes I helped frame. I was there, and you had no idea. You're coming to my store. You'll walk through my door, and I'll have to introduce myself, and then you'll know. And I don't know if you'll forgive me. I don't know if I deserve forgiveness. But I hope you'll understand that I never meant to hurt you. I only ever wanted to help.

He tore out the page, folded it, and slid it into the glove compartment with the others.

The pile was growing, too many pages filled with what should have been spoken aloud.

Nine letters. Nine confessions that never left the paper.

Sam tilted his head back against the seat and whispered to the roof of his truck, "Tomorrow. I'll tell her tomorrow. I promise."

But tomorrow will soon become today.

And he was out of time.

CHAPTER 7: Turner's Books

HOPE

Hope woke in the hotel room to a wash of watery sunlight and the sound of a car alarm having an existential crisis in the parking lot. She lay still for a moment, disoriented, before remembering: La Crosse. Lily's apartment. Today.

Her phone showed two messages.

Rebecca: *How'd you sleep? Remember, five things you can see, four you can touch. Call if you need grounding. Love you.*

And from her friend: *Good morning. Text me anything, anytime. I'm here.*

Hope typed back: *Slept okay. Currently being serenaded by a car alarm that won't give up.*

The response came immediately: *That's the spirit. Persistence in the face of futility. Very Wisconsin.*

Hope smiled. *Is that what we're known for?*

That and cheese. Mostly cheese.

Hope got up, showered, and dressed in jeans and the sweater Lily had bought her two Christmases ago, the one Lily had said made her look "like a mom from a Hallmark movie, but in a good way."

She texted Jenna: *On my way. Should I bring coffee?*

Jenna: *God, yes. And donuts. We're honoring Lily's memory through* 糖.

Through what?

My phone auto corrected to Chinese. I meant SUGAR. Bring sugar.

Hope stopped at a drive-through and ordered three large coffees and a dozen donuts. The teenager at the window looked at the order and said, "Rough morning?"

"Something like that," Hope said.

"The donuts help," the kid said sagely. "They always do."

Hope drove through campus following GPS directions, past brick buildings and students who looked impossibly young.

Was Lily ever that young? Had she walked these paths, sat on those benches, worried about finals and boys and what to do with her life?

The apartment building was old, not charming old, just old with peeling paint and a front door that didn't quite close all the way. Hope climbed the stairs to the second floor, balancing coffee, and donuts, and knocked on Apartment 2C.

The door flew open.

Jenna stood there in yoga pants and an over sized sweatshirt that read RUNNING IS A GREAT WAY TO REALIZE YOU HATE RUNNING. Her hair was in a messy bun. She looked tired but smiled when she saw Hope.

"You brought offerings," Jenna said. "Thank God. I was worried we'd have to do this sober."

"The donuts are caffeinated?" Hope asked.

"No, but they should be. Someone should invent that." Jenna took the coffee carrier. "Sheridan! Hope's here and she brought the good stuff!"

Sheridan appeared from somewhere in the back, athletic shorts, tank top, ponytail, and immediately went in for a hug, the kind that lasted longer than polite, the kind that felt like she was trying to hold them both together.

"I'm so glad you're here," Sheridan said into Hope's shoulder.

"Me too," Hope said and meant it.

The apartment was exactly what you'd expect from three twenty-year-olds living together: chaotic but charming. Mismatched furniture. Posters on the walls. A spice rack that had once been organized alphabetically and then clearly sabotaged paprika next to salt, cumin beside oregano. Pure anarchy.

"Welcome to Casa de Chaos," Jenna said, gesturing grandly. "We'd give you the tour, but you can see everything from here."

It was true. The apartment was small, with a living room, kitchenette, bathroom, and three bedrooms off a short hallway.

"Lily's room is at the end," Sheridan said softly. "We haven't changed anything."

Hope nodded. She wasn't ready for that yet. "Show me your rooms first?"

Jenna perked up. "You want to see my disaster of a life? Okay, but no judgment."

Jenna's room was actually pretty organized, bed made, and desk neat. The only chaos was the collection of running shoes lined along one wall, at least ten pairs in various stages of destruction.

"I have a problem," Jenna said, following Hope's gaze. "I keep thinking the next pair will make me enjoy running. Spoiler: they don't."

"Why do you keep running?" Hope asked.

"Because I paid for all these shoes, and I'm not a quitter." Jenna picked up a neon-green pair. These were a mistake. They glow in the dark. Do you know how terrifying it is to look down while running at night and see your own feet glowing like radioactive stumps?"

Hope laughed really, the sound surprising her.

"There it is!" Jenna grinned. "You have the best laugh. Lily always teased that it sounds like wind chimes, but warmer."

Hope's throat tightened. "She said that?"

"All the time. She'd call you and come back smiling, like she'd just talked to her favorite person in the world." Jenna set the shoes down. "Because she had."

They moved to Sheridan's room next. This one looked like a gym had exploded: yoga mat, resistance bands, foam roller, sports gear everywhere.

"I know, I know," Sheridan said. "I'm a walking cliché. Future gym teacher and all."

"It's not a cliché if you love it," Hope said.

"I do love it. I love making people move. Lily used to say I was like a golden retriever with a whistle, just happy someone wanted to play." Sheridan picked up a jump rope. "She'd work out with me sometimes. Well, 'work out' is generous. She'd do three squats, declare herself done, and eat a donut."

"That sounds right," Hope said.

"Once she tried to do a plank. Made it eight seconds and said, 'This is violence. Core muscles are a myth. I'm going to read instead. Sheridan's smile wavered. "God, I miss her."

"Me too," Hope whispered.

They drifted back to the living room and sat on the mismatched couch, Jenna on one end, Sheridan on the other,

Hope in the middle. The coffee was still hot. The donuts sat unopened on the table.

"Okay," Jenna said. "Before we go into her room, we need to prepare you."

"For what?"

"For the fact that Lily was secretly a chaos goblin disguised as an organized English major."

Sheridan giggled. "Oh my God, remember the tape?"

"The tape," Jenna said, with the gravity of someone recounting a war story. "Hope your daughter owned three! Different types of tape. Regular tape. Washi tape with little flowers. And this weird brown packing tape she claimed was 'for emergencies.'"

"What kind of emergency requires packing tape?" Hope asked.

"Exactly!" Jenna threw up her hands. "We asked! She said, 'You'll know when it happens.' It never happened! We still have the tape!"

"Show her the socks," Sheridan said.

"Oh God, the socks." Jenna was laughing now. "Lily believed, and I cannot stress this enough, believed that matching socks were a conspiracy by Big Laundry."

"Big Laundry?" Hope repeated.

"Her words! She said matching socks were a capitalist plot to make people buy more socks. She'd wear one polka-dot sock and one striped sock and call it 'fashion anarchy.'"

Hope was laughing now, the kind of laugh that came from deep in her stomach. "She wore mismatched socks in high school, too. I thought she'd grow out of it."

"Nope!" Sheridan said cheerfully. "She doubled down. Sometimes she'd wear three socks, two on one foot, one on the other. Said it kept her humble."

"How does that keep you humble?"

"We never figured that out either!"

They dissolved into laughter, the three of them on the couch, holding coffee and remembering the girl who'd connected them.

"She left notes everywhere," Jenna said, wiping her eyes. "Like, everywhere. We'd find them in the fridge, on the bathroom mirror. Once she stuck a note on Sheridan's dumbbell that said, 'You're doing great, but also, why?'"

Sheridan snorted. "I kept that note! It's still on the dumbbell!"

"She alphabetized our spices," Jenna continued. "Spent an entire afternoon organizing them. We waited until she went to class and put them all backwards just to see what she'd do."

"What did she do?" Hope asked.

"She pretended not to notice," Sheridan said. "But we heard her in the kitchen at two a.m. Fixing every single one. Then she left us a note: 'I know what you did. I'm not angry. Just disappointed. Also, basil goes before cayenne, you heathens.'"

Hope was crying now, but laughing too. "That's my girl."

"She really was the best of us," Jenna said quietly. "The glue. The one who remembered everyone's birthday, texted to make sure we'd eaten, and left encouraging notes in our textbooks during finals."

"She left notes in my anatomy textbook," Sheridan said. "Right in the middle of the section on bones. The note said, 'You've got this. You're calcium-strong.'"

"That's terrible," Hope said.

"It was perfect," Sheridan said.

They sat in a comfortable silence for a moment. Then Jenna stood and brushed powdered sugar off her sweatshirt.

"Okay," she said. "Ready?"

Hope took a breath. "Ready."

Lily's room was exactly what Hope had pictured and nothing like it at all.

The bed was unmade, sheets twisted, the pillow still dented from the last time Lily's head had rested there. Textbooks were stacked on the desk and a bag of sour gummy worms (of course).

But it was the sticky notes that broke Hope's heart.

They covered the mirror like a second reflection:

Paper due Friday, don't panic

Call Mom on Wednesday

Remember, joy is a muscle

Book a Rescue meeting on Thursday at 3 p.m.

You are allowed to be here

Basil before cayenne, Jenna

Hope touched that last one and laughed through tears. "She really did care about the spices."

"She had her priorities," Jenna said. "Books, Mom, spices in that order."

The room smelled faintly of Lily's shampoo, something floral and young that made Hope's chest ache. Plants, in need of water, leaned toward the single window. A thrift-store lamp sat on the nightstand, its shade hand-decorated with tiny stars.

"She did that the first week we moved in," Sheridan said, pointing to the lamp. "Said the room needed more magic."

Hope sat on the edge of the unmade bed and looked around. This was where Lily had slept, studied, laughed with her friends, probably cried over exams, and made plans for a future that would never come.

"Tell me about living with her," Hope said. "The everyday stuff, the things I wouldn't know."

Jenna and Sheridan settled on the floor, backs against the wall like they used to during late-night gossip sessions.

"She sang in the shower," Jenna said. "Badly. Like, aggressively badly. We're talking full Disney villain, belt-it-out energy."

"She'd do the voice and everything," Sheridan added. "I recorded her once singing 'Poor Unfortunate Souls' from The Little Mermaid. It was... it was art. Terrible art."

"She cooked exactly one meal," Jenna said. "Mac and cheese. But she was really good at it, added garlic, real cheese, sometimes vegetables if she was feeling fancy."

"We called it Lily's Chaos Mac," Sheridan said. "Because every time was different. Once she put Hot Cheetos in it."

"How was it?" Hope asked.

"Horrifying," Jenna said. "But we ate it anyway because she looked so proud."

"She'd leave books everywhere," Sheridan said. "Coffee table, kitchen counter, bathroom. We'd follow the book trail to find her."

"She talked to herself while reading," Jenna said. "Full conversations. We'd hear her in here going, 'No, don't go in there, that's obviously a trap.' Or 'KISS HIM, YOU FOOL.'"

Hope laughed. "She did that at home, too. I thought she'd grow out of it."

"Instead, she grew into it," Sheridan said. "Started doing character voices. It was like living with a one-woman audio book."

They started packing slowly, carefully. Clothes went into boxes, books into milk crates someone had "borrowed" from behind the grocery store. Each item was a decision: keep, donate, or save for Hope.

Hope found Lily's favorite sweatshirt, the one she'd "borrowed" years ago and never returned. Hope held it to her face and breathed in.

"Keep that one," Jenna said gently. "She wore it all the time. Said it smelled like home."

Hope tucked it into her bag.

They found a grocery list in Lily's handwriting:

Milk

Pasta

Garlic bread

 Chocolate

Mac and cheese

And at the bottom, in a different pen: Call Mom.

Hope pressed the list to her chest. Some things she still couldn't let go of

In the desk drawer, Sheridan found a stack of index cards. "The Book Rescue cards," she said reverently.

Hope took one:

Kent Haruf – for when quiet is the only thing that doesn't hurt.

Another:

The Night Circus – for when the world needs to be strange on purpose.

Another:

Eleanor Oliphant – for when you forget, people can be good.

"She was going to save people with these," Hope said.

"She already did," Jenna said softly. "We found notes from students who'd discovered her quote cards. They wrote back. Said her words helped them survive."

Hope looked at her daughter's careful handwriting and felt something shift in her chest. Not healing. Not yet. But maybe the first small movement toward acceptance proved that Lily's impact hadn't ended with her death.

"Can I keep these?" Hope asked.

"Of course," Sheridan said. "They're yours. They were always meant for you anyway."

They found a photo of the three of them on apartment move-in day last summer: sweaty, laughing, surrounded by boxes. Lily stood in the middle, arms around both friends, face split in a grin that said this was the best day of her life.

"She was so happy," Hope whispered.

"She was," Jenna said. "We all were. Getting this apartment felt like... I don't know. Like proof we were real adults. Like we'd made it."

"She talked about you constantly," Sheridan said. "Texted you every five minutes. We'd be watching a movie, and she'd pause it to send you a meme. Drove Jenna crazy."

"It did not!" Jenna protested. "Okay, it did a little. But it was also adorable. She'd show us your replies and get this look on her face like you'd just told her she'd won the lottery."

Hope's throat closed up. "I miss those texts."

"We know," Sheridan said gently. "We miss them too."

Around one p.m. they took a break, ordered pizza, and ate it on the living room floor surrounded by half-packed boxes.

"This feels wrong," Jenna said, gesturing at the boxes. "Packing her up. Like we're erasing her."

"We're not erasing her," Hope said. "We're... redistributing her. Letting her things go to places they'll be loved."

"That's very Zen," Jenna said. "Lily would've said something like that and then immediately eaten an entire bag of sour gummy worms to balance it out."

"Speaking of which," Sheridan said, holding up the half-eaten bag from Lily's desk. "Should we finish these? For her?"

"They're probably stale," Jenna said.

"They're definitely stale," Hope said. "Let's do it anyway."

They each took a handful, chewed, and winced.

"These are terrible," Sheridan said.

"The worst," Jenna agreed.

"Lily would've loved that we did this," Hope said.

They finished the bag.

By two-thirty, Lily's room was mostly packed, the bed stripped, the desk cleared, the sticky notes carefully removed and saved in a Ziploc bag.

The three of them stood in the doorway, looking at the space.

"It's weird," Sheridan said. "I can still feel her here."

"Me too," Jenna said.

"Maybe that's how it works," Hope said quietly. "The spaces we love keep holding us even after we're gone."

They hugged long and hard, the kind of hug that says we survived this together.

"What are you doing now?" Jenna asked.

"I want to see Turner's Books," Hope said. "The place she loved."

"Sam's great," Sheridan said. "He was really kind to her. Like a dad."

Hope's heart skipped. "You've met him?"

"A few times. Lily took us there once. He let us study upstairs for free, brought us coffee, didn't even charge us for the books Lily kept annotating."

"He stocked Diet Coke just for her," Jenna added. "Lily said it was the most romantic thing a man had ever done. We told her that was a low bar. She said it was a perfect bar."

Hope smiled. "What's he like?"

"Quiet," Sheridan said. "In a good way. Like he's listening even when you're not talking."

"Older," Jenna added. "Silver hair. Looks like he's read every book ever written and has opinions about all of them."

"Lily wanted you to meet him," Sheridan said. "Talked about it constantly. Said you two would either fall in love or argue about books for hours. Either way, she wanted to watch."

Hope's chest tightened. "She really said that?"

"Every single week," Jenna said. "She had a whole plan that was going to invite you both to some campus thing and 'accidentally' seat you next to each other."

"Subtle," Hope said.

"Lily was many things," Jenna said. "Subtle was not one of them."

Hope hugged them both again. "Thank you. For loving her. For being her family."

"She was ours too," Sheridan said

Hope drove to downtown La Crosse with the windows down and Lily's playlist on shuffle. The song that came up first was 'Dancing Queen.'

Hope almost skipped it. But she didn't.

She let it play, sang along badly, and let the grief and joy exist in the same breath.

Three inches to the left, she thought. Maybe she was getting there.

Turner's Books sat on a corner lot, its red door bright against the old brick. The sign above read exactly what Hope had seen online:

TURNER'S BOOKS-NEW, USED, AND NECESSARY

Hope parked across the street and sat in the car, gathering courage.

Her phone buzzed.

Her friend: How's it going?

Hope typed: *Just finished packing the apartment. Going to the bookstore now, the one I told you about.*

Turner's?

Yes. I'm nervous.

Why?

I don't know. It feels important. Seeing this place will make her more real.

She was real. The place will just show you another side of her.

That's what I'm afraid of. What if I don't recognize that side?

You will. A mother always knows her daughter, even the parts she couldn't see.

Hope read that three times, then took a breath. *Okay. Going in now.*

Text me after. I want to hear about it.

I will.

Hope got out of the car, crossed the street, and stopped in front of the red door.

Through the window, she could see warm light, shelves crowded with books, and a counter near the back. Behind it stood a man tall, with gray hair and a streak at his temple, quiet eyes. He was helping a customer, wrapping a book in brown paper with careful hands.

Hope's heart stopped.

That was him. That was Sam.

The man Lily had tried to set her up with the bookstore owner who'd stocked Diet Coke, let her daughter study for free, and created a space where Lily felt safe enough to leave words for strangers.

Hope pushed open the door.

The bell chimed, soft and welcoming. The smell hit her immediately: old paper, coffee, and something sweet, maybe cinnamon.

Sam looked up from the counter. Their eyes met.

For a moment, neither of them moved.

Then Sam smiled slightly, carefully, and kindly said, "Welcome to Turner's. Let me know if you need help finding anything."

His voice. Hope knew that voice.

Not from meeting him before. She'd never met him before.

But she knew it anyway.

From somewhere. From...

No.

It wasn't possible.

Hope's mouth opened, but no words came.

Sam's smile faltered. "Are you all right?"

"I'm ..." Hope tried to find her footing. "I'm Hope. Hope Hawthorne. I was . . ."

"Lily's mother," Sam finished softly. He came around the counter. "I'm so sorry for your loss. Your daughter was a remarkable person."

Hope watched his face, the careful way he held himself, the sadness in his eyes that suggested his grief was personal, not just sympathetic.

"You knew her," Hope said.

"I did. She came here often. Studied upstairs." Sam gestured toward the stairs. "Would you like to see the space where she spent so much time?"

Hope nodded, unable to speak.

She followed him up the narrow stairs. The second floor was quieter, with more intimate poetry, literary fiction, and classics. And in the corner, by the window:

A leather chair, worn soft, with good light falling just so.

"She sat here," Sam said. "For hours. I'd bring her a Diet Coke. She'd leave quotes in books. She made this place better just by being in it."

Hope walked to the chair and sat down. The leather was cool; the view perfect, the street below, the sky above, the world at just the right distance.

"The light," Hope whispered.

"Good light," Sam agreed. "It stays longer than you think."

Hope's head snapped up.

Good light.

That phrase.

She'd heard it before in a text message. From . . .

She pulled out her phone with shaking hands, opened the thread, and found the message from last week:

The light is kind there. It stays longer than you think.

She looked up at Sam. He stood by the stairs, hands in his pockets, face carefully neutral.

"Did you ..." Hope's voice shook. "Did you help set up her memorial? At the library?"

Sam's throat worked. "Yes."

"The chair. The books. The way the light falls."

"Yes."

"You built that. For her."

"For her," Sam said quietly. "And for everyone who needed what she gave."

Hope stood, walked toward him, and stopped three feet away.

"The texts," she said. "The person I've been texting. The friend who's been helping me."

Sam closed his eyes. "Hope ..."

"It's you," she said. "Isn't it?"

Sam opened his eyes and met her gaze. And in his expression, she saw everything: the guilt, the grief, the desperate desire to help, the cowardice that had kept him silent.

"It's you," Hope said again.

Sam nodded once. "It's me. I'm so sorry. I should have told you from the beginning. I . . ."

She looked down at the phone in her hand.

Opened the messages from her friend, from Sam, sent before he knew that she knew:

I hope the bookstore is everything you needed it to be. Text me when you're ready to talk.

Hope looked from the phone to Sam, from the words on the screen to the man who'd written them.

And then, impossibly, she laughed.

Not a bitter laugh. Not an angry one. Just.. a laugh. The sound of absurdity, meeting relief, meeting grief, meeting something she didn't have a name for yet.

"You texted me," Hope said. "While I'm standing in your bookstore."

Sam looked stricken. "I didn't know you were. I just wanted to."

"Stop," Hope said. She held up her hand and took a breath. "Just... stop."

Sam stopped.

Her hands were shaking now. She couldn't think.

Hope walks downstairs and right out the door. Sam watches her as she leaves.

I need to call Rebecca, she thought.

Hope tried to figure out if she was furious or grateful or some impossible combination of both.

After what felt like forever, she walks back inside the bookstore and finds Sam staring at her. He was trying to read her face.

"We need to talk," Hope said finally.

"Yes," Sam agreed. "We do."

"But not here. Somewhere else. Somewhere neutral."

"There's a coffee shop two blocks away," Sam said. "Good coffee. Quiet."

"Okay."

Hope headed for the stairs, then stopped and turned back.

"For what it's worth," she said softly, "the texts helped. You helped. Even if you should've told me who you were."

"I know," Sam said quietly. "I'm sorry I didn't."

Hope nodded once and went downstairs. Sam followed.

At the counter, Hope paused and looked around the store, the shelves Lily had browsed, the front table where she'd discovered new books, the sign that said NECESSARY like it was the most important word in the language.

"She loved this place," Hope said.

"I loved having her here," Sam said.

Hope looked at him, really looked at him. At the gray streak in his hair. The careful way he held himself. The grief etched into the lines around his eyes.

He'd lost someone, too. His wife, probably. The bookstore had been her dream.

And then he'd lost Lily, the girl who'd reminded him why the dream mattered.

And then he'd found Hope. Or maybe Hope had found him. And instead of telling her who he was, he'd just helped in the only way he knew how.

It was wrong.

But it was also human.

"Two blocks away?" Hope asked.

"Two blocks," Sam confirmed. "I can close the store for an hour."

"Okay."

Hope pulled out her phone and typed:

I know it's you. Meet me at the coffee shop in ten minutes. We need to talk.

She hit send and watched Sam's phone buzz in his pocket.

He pulled it out, read the message, then looked up at her with something like relief in his eyes.

"Ten minutes," he said.

Hope nodded and walked out of Turner's Books into the gray afternoon, heart pounding, hands shaking, mind racing with everything she needed to say to the man who'd been her bridge without her knowing.

The man Lily had chosen for her.

The man who'd kept a secret but told the truth in every other way.

Hope got into her car and sat there for a long moment, trying to organize her thoughts into something that made sense.

Her phone buzzed.

Sam: *I'm closing up now. I'll meet you there. And Hope? Thank you for giving me a chance to explain.*

Hope looked at the message, then at the bookstore across the street, where Sam was probably locking the door, his hands shaking as badly as hers.

She typed: *Ten minutes. And bring tissues. I think we're both going to need them.*

Then she started the car and drove two blocks to the coffee shop, where everything would finally come into the light.

CHAPTER 8: The Weight of Knowing

Late May, La Crosse – Coffee shop

SAM

Sam locked the front door of Turner's with hands that wouldn't stop shaking. He flipped the sign to "CLOSED," pulled the shade, and stood in the dim store, trying to remember how to breathe.

She knew.

Hope knew.

The bridge had a name and a face, and she was two blocks away, waiting for an explanation he didn't know how to give.

Sam pulled out his phone and stared at the thread of those blue and gray bubbles, two weeks of careful comfort built on omission.

He opened his confession notebook one last time, flipping through pages of unsent truths, the stack of folded papers that should have been honest words.

He wrote one more:

I'm about to tell you everything. I don't know if you'll forgive me, but I hope you'll understand that every word I sent you was true, even if I was too afraid to attach my name to them.

He tore out the page, folded it, and slipped it into his pocket instead of the drawer.

This confession he'd give her in person.

Sam grabbed his coat, turned off the lights, and walked into the gray afternoon toward a conversation he should have had two weeks ago.

The coffee shop was called The Daily Grind, an unoriginal name, a terrible pun, but excellent coffee. Sam had been coming here for years. The owner, Margaret, knew his order by heart: black coffee, no sugar, and, occasionally, a scone if he was having a particularly rough day.

Today felt like a scone day. Maybe two.

Hope was already there, sitting at a corner table by the window. She had a mug in front of her, and by the look of it, her hands wrapped around it like she was trying to absorb its warmth.

Sam stopped at the counter.

"Black coffee," he told Margaret. "And two scones."

"Two?" Margaret raised an eyebrow. "That bad a day?"

"Worse," Sam said.

"Want to talk about it?"

"I'm about to," Sam said, nodding toward Hope.

Margaret followed his gaze. "That the woman whose daughter…?"

"Yeah."

Margaret's expression softened. "Take the back table if you need more privacy. And, Sam, whatever you did, just tell her the truth. It's the only thing that helps."

Sam nodded and carried his coffee to Hope's table, setting the scones between them like a peace offering.

"You brought scones," Hope said.

"I brought scones," Sam confirmed. "I didn't know if you'd want one, but they're here. Just in case."

Hope almost smiled. Almost.

Sam sat down across from her. For a moment, neither of them spoke, just sat in the particular quiet of two people trying to figure out where to start.

Finally, Hope said, "When?"

"When did I know it was you?"

"When did you decide to lie to me?"

Sam flinched. "I didn't decide it, just… happened. And then I didn't know how to un-happen it."

"Walk me through it," Hope said. Her voice was steady, controlled. Not angry yet, but not not angry either.

"From the beginning."

Sam took a breath. "I got a new phone last month. New carrier, new number. The old one wouldn't hold a charge anymore." He paused. "It had all my wife's voicemails. Her texts. I kept it as long as I could."

Hope's expression flickered understanding, maybe. Or sympathy. "I'm sorry."

"Thank you." Sam wrapped his hands around his coffee mug. "The new number was random, just whatever the carrier had available. And then on May eleventh"

"Lily's birthday."

"Your message came through. *Happy birthday, baby. I miss you so much.*" Sam's throat tightened. "At first, I thought it was just a wrong number. But the date… Lily's birthday… I put it together pretty quickly."

"And you responded anyway."

"I should have just said wrong number, sorry, but I couldn't. I've been where you were wanting so badly to reach someone who's gone. Texting them anyway, even knowing it's pointless." He looked at Hope. "If someone had answered me those first months after Elise died, even by accident, I don't know. It might have helped."

Hope absorbed that. "So you responded. I'm listening."

Hope's jaw tightened. "You could have told me who you were."

"I know."

"You could have said, I'm Sam Turner. I own Turner's Books. I knew your daughter."

"I know."

"But you didn't.

"I didn't."

"Why?"

Sam had practiced this answer a dozen times in his head, had written it down, crossed it out, rewritten it. But now, looking at Hope's face at the hurt, confusion, and desperate need to understand, all his practiced words deserted him.

"Because I was a coward," he said simply. "And because I was selfish."

Hope blinked. "Selfish?"

"The texts weren't just helping you," Sam said. "They were helping me, too. Every time I wrote back, I felt closer to Lily, like I was honoring her memory. Continuing her work of saving people with words." He looked down at his coffee. "I needed that. Needed to feel useful again. Needed to feel like maybe I could still do some good."

"So you let me believe you were a stranger."

"Yes."

"Let me pour my heart out to someone I thought I'd never meet."

"Yes."

"Let me think, I was texting some kind stranger instead of the man my daughter tried to set me up with."

Sam's head snapped up. "You knew about that?"

"Jenna and Sheridan told me. Today." Hope's voice was tight. "Lily talked about you constantly. Had a whole plan to introduce us. She was excited about it."

Sam closed his eyes. "She talked about you, too, all the time. How much she loved you. How she worried you were lonely. How she wanted you to unfold that was her word. Unfold."

Hope's heart took a leap.

"I should have told you," Sam continued. "That first day. That first message when I knew. I should have said, I'm the bookstore owner. I knew Lily. But I thought… I don't know what I thought. Maybe you needed the anonymity. That maybe knowing would make it harder."

"That's not your decision to make," Hope said quietly.

"You're right. It wasn't."

They sat in silence. Around them, the coffee shop kept its ordinary rhythm: espresso machine hissing, mugs clinking, people laughing at other tables about things that didn't involve grief, or lies, or impossible situations.

"When did you realize?" Sam asked. "That it was me?"

"Today. Just now." Hope took a sip of tea. "The phrase' good light. You said it at the bookstore, and I remembered you'd texted it before. About the memorial corner."

Sam nodded. "I tried to be careful not to give myself away. But I kept slipping."

"The word necessary," Hope said. "You used it in a text. Same word that's on your sign."

"I know."

"And when I asked if you knew her, you said you 'knew of her.' Past tense. Not 'know of.' Knew."

"I was trying not to lie outright," Sam said. "Trying to stay technically honest while still hiding."

"That's just lying with extra steps," Hope said.

Sam couldn't argue with that.

"What were you going to do?" Hope asked. "If I hadn't figured it out? Just keep texting me forever? Let me visit the bookstore and never connect the dots?"

"I was going to tell you today," Sam said. "When you came to the store. I'd decided no more hiding."

"Really?" Hope's skepticism was clear.

Sam pulled the folded paper from his pocket, the tenth confession. He unfolded it and slid it across the table.

Hope picked it up and read it. Her expression shifted, anger softening into something more complicated.

"You wrote this before I figured it out," she said.

"Just now. Before I left the store."

Hope refolded the paper carefully. "You have others like this?"

"Nine others. In my register drawer at the store. Things I should have said but wrote down instead."

"Nine times you almost told me the truth."

"Nine times I was too afraid."

Hope set the paper down and looked out the window at the street beyond. "I don't know if I'm angry or grateful or both."

"Both are allowed," Sam said quietly.

"Is it? Can I be furious that you lied and also relieved that you were there? Can I feel betrayed and thankful at the same time?"

"Yes," Sam said. "Grief taught me that. You can hold two truths at once; they don't cancel each other out."

Hope looked at him, then really looked at him. At the gray streak in his hair, the grief lines around his eyes, the way he held himself like someone who'd learned to be careful with the world.

"You loved her," Hope said, not a question.

"Not the way you did," Sam said quickly. "Not as a parent. But yes. She reminded me why I keep the store open. Why books matter. Why kindness matters. She made me feel less alone."

"And when she died?"

"I went to the funeral. Stood in the back. Saw you in the front row." Sam's voice dropped. "You looked exactly how I felt when Elise died. Like someone had taken the floor away, and you were just… floating. Waiting to crash."

"That's exactly how it felt," Hope whispered.

"I wanted to talk to you then to tell you how much Lily meant to me. But it didn't feel like my place. I was just the bookstore owner. One of dozens of people she'd touched."

"You were more than that," Hope said. "The girls told me. She saw you as a father figure, the kind of dad she wished she'd had."

Sam's eyes went bright. He blinked rapidly. "I didn't know she felt that way."

"David was never really there," Hope said. "Even before the divorce. He was checked out, more interested in his career, his new life. Lily needed someone who saw her. Who listened. Who cared about the things she cared about." She paused. "That was you."

Sam had to look away. "I should have told you that. Should have introduced myself at the funeral. But I was grieving too, and I didn't know how to do it publicly. So I just… left."

"And then I texted you."

"And then you texted me. And I thought, just for a moment, that maybe this was Lily's way of making sure we met after all. That maybe she'd orchestrated this somehow."

Hope's mouth twisted into something that wasn't quite a smile. "That sounds like something she'd do."

"She was always trying to fix people," Sam said. "To save them. Leave the right words in the right place at the right time."

"The quote cards," Hope said.

"I kept one." Sam pulled out his wallet. Tucked inside was a laminated index card in Lily's handwriting:

You have to remember that goodness is more powerful than evil… And that love is stronger than hate – Kent Haruf

Hope took it with shaking hands, tracing the words with her finger. "She left this for you?"

"In a book upstairs. The week before she died." Sam's voice was rough. "I read it every day when the grief felt too big, when I didn't know if I could keep going. It helped."

"She had a whole box of these," Hope said. "For her Book Rescue project."

"I know. I helped frame some of them for the memorial corner."

Hope looked up sharply. "You were there. At the dedication ceremony."

"Yes."

"And you saw me."

"Yes."

"And you texted me while I was standing there looking at the memorial you built."

Sam's face crumpled. "I'm sorry. I know how that sounds. I know how wrong it was. I just… didn't know how to do anything else."

Hope pressed her palms against her eyes. "This is so messed up."

"I know."

"You helped me. For weeks, you kept me alive. Gave me a reason to get up. Made me feel less alone."

"I hope that's true."

"It is true." Hope dropped her hands. "But you also lied by omission, by hiding, by letting me believe something that wasn't real."

"The comfort was real," Sam said urgently. "Every word I sent you was true. I just didn't attach my name to it."

"That's what makes it so complicated," Hope said. "If you'd been cruel, I could just be angry. If you'd been honest from the start, I could just be grateful. But you were kind and dishonest, and I don't know how to hold both those things."

"I don't either," Sam admitted.

They sat in heavy silence. Sam's coffee had gone cold. Hope's tea was probably the same. The scones sat untouched between them like a failed peace treaty.

"What now?" Hope asked finally.

"I don't know."

"That's honest, at least."

Sam almost smiled. "I'm trying to be honest now. Better late than never."

"Is it better late," Hope asked, "or is late just… late?"

Sam didn't have an answer for that.

Hope pulled out her phone, opened the thread, and scrolled through the messages- weeks of blue and gray, of comfort and kindness, of words that had kept her breathing.

"I don't want to lose this," Hope said quietly. "The connection. The person who helped me. Even if that person isn't who I thought they were."

"You don't have to lose it," Sam said. "I'm still me. I just have a name now."

"But it changes things," Hope said. "Before, you were just a voice. A bridge. Now you're a person with a face, with history with my daughter, with your own grief. It's complicated."

"Complicated isn't impossible," Sam said.

Hope looked at him. "No. But it's not simple either."

"I don't need simple," Sam said. "I just need… something. Some way forward. Some chance to prove that I was trying to help, not hurt."

Hope set her phone down. "Tell me about Elise."

Sam blinked. "What?"

"Your wife. The one who wanted a bookstore. Tell me about her."

Sam wasn't sure what this had to do with anything, but he answered anyway. "She loved books the way other people love oxygen, couldn't imagine a life without them. We met at an estate sale, both reaching for the same vintage poetry collection."

"Who got it?"

"I did. But I promised to discuss it with her." He smiled at the memory. "She said, 'You can have the book if you take me to coffee and tell me why Hopkins matters.' So I did."

"And?"

"And she was brilliant. Funny. Had opinions about everything. We were married six months later."

"Fast," Hope said.

"When you know, you know," Sam said. "Or at least, I thought I knew. Turns out you never really know. Life always has one more surprise."

"Cancer?" Hope asked gently.

"Stage four. By the time they found it, there wasn't much they could do. We bought the bookstore during her remission, her dream. We ran it together for eight months before..." He trailed off.

"Before she died," Sam confirmed. "Two years ago. Two years, three months, and sixteen days."

"You're counting.

"I'm always counting."

Hope reached across the table and covered his hand with hers just for a moment, just long enough to say *I understand.*

"That's why I kept the store open," Sam said. "It was her dream. I couldn't let it die just because she had."

"And then Lily showed up."

"And then Lily showed up," Sam agreed. "With her Diet Coke and her books and her way of making the world feel less empty. She reminded me why Elise wanted this place, why books matter. Why people matter."

"And when she died?"

"It felt like losing Elise again," Sam said. "Like the universe was taking away everyone who made life bearable."

"And then I texted you," Hope said.

"And then you texted me. And for the first time in months, I felt useful again, like maybe I could help someone the way Lily had helped me."

Hope pulled her hand back. "So you helped. But you also hid."

"Yes."

"And now I'm supposed to decide if the help outweighs the hiding."

"I'm not asking you to decide anything," Sam said. "I'm just trying to explain. To give you the whole truth. Finally."

Hope picked up one of the scones, broke off a piece, and ate it without tasting it.

"These are good," she said absently.

"They're Margaret's specialty. Blueberry with lemon zest."

"Lily would have liked them."

"She did. She'd come in after studying and order two, claiming she needed the sugar to recover from academic trauma."

Hope's mouth quirked. "That sounds like her."

They sat for a while. The coffee shop hummed around them. Eventually, Margaret came by with fresh coffee and tea.

"Refills," she said quietly. "On the house."

"Thank you," Hope said.

After Margaret left, Hope looked at Sam. "I need time."

"Of course."

"I need to think about this. About what it means. About whether I can trust you after you hid who you were."

"I understand."

"But I don't want to stop talking to you," Hope said. "That's the part I'm stuck on. I'm angry, but I also don't want to lose the bridge. Does that make sense?"

"Perfect sense," Sam said.

"So maybe we try this," Hope said. "Maybe we keep talking, but honestly, this time. No more hiding. No more omissions."

"I can do that."

"And maybe I will visit the bookstore again. Sit in Lily's chair. Get to know the place she loved."

"I'd like that."

"And maybe we figure out how to be friends. Real friends. Not just text-message friends."

Sam felt something in his chest loosen. "I'd like that too."

Hope finished her tea. Sam finished his coffee. The scones disappeared between them.

When they stood to leave, Hope said, "Can I ask you something?"

"Anything."

"The memorial corner. When you were building it, what were you thinking?"

Sam considered. "I was thinking that Lily deserved a space that felt like her. That honored her love of books, light, and quiet. That gave people what she'd given me: a place to breathe."

"And?"

"And I was thinking about you. About how you'd probably visit it someday. And I wanted it to be perfect. Wanted you to see how much she was loved."

Hope's eyes went bright. "Thank you for that. It was perfect."

"You're welcome."

They walked out of the coffee shop together and stood on the sidewalk in the gray afternoon.

"Where are you parked?" Sam asked.

"Two blocks that way." Hope pointed.

"I'll walk with you."

They walked in comfortable silence. When they reached Hope's car, she turned to face him.

"Sam?"

"Yes?"

"The texts helped. Even if you should have told me who you were, they helped. I want you to know that."

"Thank you," Sam said quietly.

"And I'm glad I know now. Glad you have a name and a face and a story. It makes the help more real somehow."

"I'm glad too."

Hope unlocked her car and paused with her hand on the door. "I'll text you when I get home so you know I made it safely."

"I'd appreciate that."

"And Sam? Use your name this time when you respond."

Sam smiled, real, warm, relieved. "I will. I promise."

Hope got in her car and drove away. Sam stood on the sidewalk and watched her taillights disappear around the corner.

Then he pulled out his phone and typed: *Thank you for giving me a chance to explain. For not hating me. For understanding that people can be good and flawed at the same time.*

He almost hit send. Then he remembered she wasn't home yet. She was driving.

He saved it as a draft instead.

And for the first time in two weeks, Sam walked back to his bookstore with something that felt almost like peace.

HOPE

Hope drove out of La Crosse with her hands tight on the wheel and her mind full of everything Sam had said.

He'd lied by omission, by hiding, by letting her believe something that wasn't quite true.

But he'd also helped. Had been there every day, every message, every moment she needed someone.

Both things were true. Both things mattered.

Hope didn't know how to reconcile them. Didn't know if she should forgive him, stay angry, or feel some complicated mix of both.

She pulled over at a rest stop halfway home, got out, and walked to a picnic table. Sat with her phone in her hand.

She called Rebecca.

"Hey," Rebecca answered. "How'd it go?"

"I don't even know where to start," Hope said.

"Start anywhere. I've got time."

So Hope told her all of it. The apartment, the girls, the bookstore, the revelation, the coffee shop, the whole complicated truth.

When she finished, Rebecca was quiet for a long moment.

"So," Rebecca said finally, "he's the bookstore owner. The one Lily wanted you to meet."

"Yes."

"And he's been texting you for weeks without telling you who he was."

"Yes."

"And now you're trying to figure out if you're angry or grateful or both."

"Exactly."

Rebecca made a thoughtful sound. "Okay. Here's what I think. And remember, I'm your sister first, therapist second."

"Noted."

"He was wrong not to tell you," Rebecca said. "That's clear. Omission is still deception, even if the intention was good."

"I know."

"But," Rebecca continued, "he also helped you survive. Gave you support when you needed it. That's not nothing."

"I know that too."

"So the question isn't whether he was right or wrong. The question is: can you forgive him? And do you want to?"

Hope watched a family at another picnic table: parents, two kids, everyone laughing about something. Normal. Easy. Uncomplicated.

"I think I can," Hope said. "I think I do. But I'm scared."

"Of what?"

"Of trusting him. Of letting him in. Of losing someone else."

"Those are valid fears," Rebecca said. "But Hope? You're not losing anyone by talking to him. You're just adding someone. That's different."

"What if it's too complicated? What if the history with Lily makes it impossible?"

"Then you'll figure it out," Rebecca said simply. "But you won't know unless you try."

Hope smiled despite herself. "When did you get so wise?"

"I read a lot of books. Also, I'm your older sister; it's my job to sound wise."

They talked for a few more minutes. Then Hope hung up and sat in the quiet.

Her phone buzzed.

Rebecca: *Also? Lily was right. You two do sound perfect for each other. Just saying.*

Hope laughed and texted back: *Not helping.*

Rebecca: *Not trying to help. Trying to meddle. There's a difference.*

Hope put her phone away and got back in the car. The rest of the drive home was quiet, no music, just her thoughts, the road, and the slowly setting sun.

When she pulled into her driveway, the yellow house looked the same as always. But Hope felt different. Lighter, maybe. Or just… different.

She went inside, made tea, and sat at the kitchen table with her phone.

Opened the thread with Sam.

All those blue and gray bubbles. All those words that had kept her breathing.

She typed: *Made it home safely. Thank you for today. For the honesty. Finally*

The response came within seconds: *Thank you for listening. For not walking away. For giving me a chance I didn't deserve- Sam*

Hope smiled at the signature on the name that made everything real.

She typed: *We'll figure this out. One day at a time.*

One day at a time, Sam agreed. I can do that.

Good night, Sam.

Good night, Hope.

Hope set the phone down and looked around her kitchen at the yellow walls, at the window where she'd watched storms with Lily, at the table where they'd eaten breakfast every morning.

Lily wasn't here anymore. But her impact was everywhere: in the books on the shelf, in the quote cards Hope had brought home, in the bookstore owner who'd loved her enough to help her mother survive.

Hope pulled one of the quote cards from her bag and read it in Lily's handwriting:

"Stories save lives." Rebecca Solnit

"You're still saving people, baby," Hope whispered. "Even now."

She set the card on the counter where she'd see it every morning, a reminder, a promise, a bridge between who she'd been and who she was becoming.

Then she made herself dinner, actual food, not just tea, and ate it at the table while texting Sam about nothing important.

About books. About the weather. About the way light changes in spring.

Small things. Normal things. The building blocks of friendship.

And maybe, someday, something more.

But for now, friendship was enough.

For now, Hope was breathing.

And that was everything.

CHAPTER 9: Crossed Wires

Early June, three weeks after the revelation

HOPE

The texts changed after Sam's confession. Not in frequency, they still messaged daily, but in texture, the tone shifted once she knew who was behind the words.

"Good morning" became *"Good morning from Sam Turner, bookstore owner, widower, the man who'd kept Diet Coke stocked for her daughter."*

"How are you feeling?" became a question from someone with a face, a history, a grief that mirrored her own.

It was both easier and harder.

Easier because the mystery was gone, no more wondering, guessing, no more nagging feeling that she was missing something obvious.

Harder because now the connection was real, and she had to decide what to do with it.

Hope sat at her kitchen table one Wednesday morning, coffee cooling beside her laptop, and typed:

Editing a manuscript about a woman who loses her husband and finds meaning through baking. It's making me hungry and sad at the same time.

Sam's reply came a few minutes later: *That's the sign of good writing when it affects you physically. Also, what kind of baking?*

Bread, mostly. She keeps making sourdough starters and naming them.

Naming them?

Herman. Brunhilda. Kevin. She has five starters, each with distinct personalities.

That's either genius or concerning.

Both, Hope typed. *Definitely both.*

She smiled at her phone. This was easier, the lightness, the banter, the way small talk somehow carried weight.

Her phone rang. Rebecca.

"Hey," Hope answered.

"Tell me about Sam," Rebecca said without preamble. "I need an update."

"We're texting. Talking. Building a friendship."

"And?"

"And what?"

"And is there more than friendship happening?"

Hope felt her cheeks warm. "Rebecca."

"I'm asking as your sister, not your therapist. Is there chemistry? Attraction? The potential for something?"

"I don't know," Hope said honestly. "I'm still figuring out how to be friends with someone who kept a secret for weeks."

"Omitted," Rebecca corrected. "There's a difference."

"You're taking his side?"

"I'm not taking sides. I'm observing that you text him every day, smile when his name pops up, and talk about him more than you've talked about any man since David."

Hope opened her mouth, then closed it. "I do not."

"You mentioned him seventeen times in our last conversation."

"I did not wait, you counted?"

"I'm a therapist. Counting is what we do." Rebecca's voice softened. "Hope, I'm not saying you have to date him. I'm saying it's okay if you want to."

"It's too soon."

"For what? For Lily? Or for you?"

Hope didn't have an answer for that.

"Just think about it," Rebecca said. "Lily wanted you two to meet. Maybe trust her judgment."

After they hung up, Hope stared at her phone.

Seventeen times. Had she really said his name that often?

She scrolled through their text thread, watching how the messages had evolved from careful comfort to easy conversation to something that felt almost like... what? Flirting?

No. Not flirting.

Just warmth. Familiarity. Connection.

Her phone buzzed.

Sam: *Question: If you could only read one genre for the rest of your life, what would it be and why? This is for science.*

Hope: *What kind of science?*

Sam: *Bookstore science. I'm reorganizing the shelves and need to understand my customer base.*

Hope: *Your customer base is mostly college students who need textbooks and the occasional novel for English class.*

Sam: *You wound me. We're much more than that.*

Hope: *Are you?*

Sam: *We also sell coffee. And house a small colony of dust bunnies who may or may not be sentient.*

Hope laughed out loud in her empty kitchen.

Hope: *To answer your question: literary fiction. Because I like books that hurt me a little.*

Sam: *That's the most book-person answer I've ever heard.*

Hope: *What about you?*

Sam: *Poetry. Because sometimes you need the truth compressed into the smallest possible space.*

Hope: *That's the most Sam answer I've ever heard.*

Sam: *Is that good or bad?*

Hope: *Good. Definitely good.*

She set the phone down and tried to focus on editing, but her mind kept drifting to the bookstore, to the man behind the counter, to the way his eyes had looked when he confessed everything.

Guilty but honest. Afraid but brave enough to tell the truth anyway.

Her phone buzzed again.

Sam: *Would you want to do a phone call sometime? Actual voices instead of typing? No pressure. Just thought it might be nice.*

Hope's heart did something complicated.

A phone call. Real-time conversation. No time to edit her words or craft the perfect response.

It felt like a big step.

It also felt inevitable.

Hope: *Yes. I'd like that.*

Sam: *Tonight? After I close the store?*

Hope: *Tonight works.*

Sam*: 7 p.m.?*
Hope*: 7 p.m.*

Hope set her phone down and immediately panicked.

A phone call. With Sam. Tonight.

She called Rebecca back.

"He wants to talk on the phone," Hope blurted without a greeting.

"And you said yes?"

"I said yes."

"Good."

"Rebecca, what do I even talk about?"

"The same things you text about. Books. Grief. Life. Your mutual love for a girl who tried to set you up."

"That's not pressure at all."

"Hope," Rebecca said gently. "He's not calling to judge you. He's calling because he likes talking to you. Just be yourself."

"What if I'm boring?"

"Your daughter loved you. Your sister loves you. I'm guessing Sam will too. Now stop spiraling and do something that makes you happy for the next eight hours, so you're not a wreck by seven."

Hope hung up and tried to obey. She finished editing a manuscript, made lunch, walked around the block, listened to Lily's playlist without crying—progress. Took a shower. Changed clothes three times before remembering it was just a phone call.

At 6:55 p.m., she sat on the couch with her phone, heart pounding like she was sixteen again, waiting for a boy to call.

Except she wasn't sixteen. She was forty-two. And this wasn't a boy—it was a man who'd helped her survive her worst weeks.

At exactly 7:00 p.m., the phone rang.

Sam's name glowed on the screen bright, real, grounding.

She answered.

"Hello?"

"Hope." His voice, no longer mediated by text, was deeper and warmer than she'd imagined. "Hi."

"Hi," she said. Then, because her brain had apparently stopped working: "You called."

"I did. Is this weird? This feels weird."

"A little," she admitted.

"We can go back to texting if you want."

"No," Hope said quickly. "I like this. Just… adjusting."

"Me too."

They were quiet for a moment. Not awkward. Just… present.

"So," Sam said. "How was the rest of your day?"

And just like that, they were talking about her manuscript, his bookstore, about nothing and everything.

Sam told her about a student who'd asked for a book on "existential dread, but make it funny." Hope laughed so hard she snorted.

"That's amazing," Sam said.

"What is the student's request?"

"Your laugh. It's exactly how Lily described it."

Hope's throat tightened. "She told you about my laugh?"

"She said it sounded like wind chimes, but warmer. I didn't get it until just now."

They talked for an hour. Then two. At some point, Hope moved from the couch to Lily's room, curling up on the unmade bed with the phone pressed to her ear.

"Where are you?" Sam asked.

"Lily's room. I come in here sometimes, when I miss her."

"Does it help?"

"It used to hurt. Now it's more… bittersweet. Like visiting someone you love."

"That sounds like progress."

"Three inches to the left," Hope said.

"What?"

"You told me once that grief moves three inches to the left. That someday I'd wake up and be able to breathe around it. I think I'm getting there."

Sam was quiet for a moment. Then: "I'm glad."

They talked about Elise, the bookstore she'd dreamed of, the one Sam almost closed after she died, but couldn't.

"She'd haunt me," Sam said with a faint laugh. "In the nicest possible way. She'd show up in my dreams and say, 'Sam Turner, you didn't learn everything about running a bookstore just to close it now.'"

"Would you ever close it?" Hope asked. "Retire?"

"I don't know. Some days I think about it. But then a student comes in looking for the exact right book, and I find it, and they light up like I've handed them magic. And I think—okay, one more day."

"One more day," Hope echoed softly. "That's how I think about grief. Just get through one more day."

"And then you string enough days together, and suddenly it's been three months."

"Almost four now," she said. "Hard to believe."

"You're doing well," Sam said. "In case no one's told you that lately."

"Rebecca tells me constantly. But it's nice hearing it from someone else."

"You are," Sam said firmly. "You're surviving something impossible. That takes strength."

Hope pulled Lily's quilt around her shoulders. "So are you. Still running a bookstore. Still helping students. Still showing up."

"We're quite the pair," Sam said lightly. "Two people held together by books and stubbornness."

"And grief."

"And grief," Sam agreed. "Though I like to think of it as love that doesn't know where to go."

Hope's breath caught. "That's beautiful. Did you read it somewhere?"

"I don't remember. It might be mine, or maybe someone else's. At this point, all the grief quotes blur together."

They talked until Hope's phone battery dropped to twenty percent, until her voice grew hoarse, until she was lying in Lily's bed with the quilt pulled up and her eyes heavy.

"I should let you go," Sam said. "It's almost eleven."

"Is it?" Hope checked the time. "Oh my God, we've been talking for four hours."

"Was it okay? Too much?"

"It was perfect," Hope said softly. "Can we do it again?"

"Anytime you want."

They said good night. Hope plugged in her phone and stayed in Lily's bed, too comfortable to move. She fell asleep surrounded by Lily's shampoo scent and the lingering warmth of *Sam's voice, wind chimes*, only softer.

SAM

The next few weeks fell into a rhythm. Texts during the day. Phone calls at night. Sometimes just twenty minutes. Sometimes hours.

Sam learned things about Hope he'd never known from texts alone:

- She hummed while she edited, unconscious melodies rising and falling with her mood.

- She was terrible at cooking but had perfected the art of ordering takeout.

- She missed her daughter most at night when silence filled the house.

- She laughed at terrible puns and tried unsuccessfully to pretend she hadn't.

- She was thinking about going back to Lily's apartment in La Crosse, this time simply to visit.

"There's a coffee shop Lily loved," Hope said during one call. "The girls mentioned it. I thought I might go sit where she sat, drink what she drank."

"That sounds nice," Sam said. "Let me know if you want company. Or not. Whatever you need."

"Would you want to? Come with me?"

Sam's heart did something complicated and unnamable. "Yes. If you want me there."

"I think I do," Hope said.

They made plans for the following Saturday coffee at Lily's favorite shop, then maybe the bookstore afterward. Nothing heavy. Just two people existing in the same space, honoring the girl who'd once tried to connect them.

Friday morning, Hope was editing when her doorbell rang.

She wasn't expecting anyone. Rebecca was in California; Jenna and Sheridan were in La Crosse; Sam was at the bookstore.

She opened the door.

Sheriff Martinez stood on the porch, hat in hand, expression solemn enough to make Hope's stomach drop.

"Mrs. Hawthorne," he said. "May I come in?"

Hope stepped aside, déjà vu washing over her. The last time he'd stood in this hallway, he'd told her Lily was dead. What could be worse than that? Friday morning, Hope was editing when her doorbell rang.

She wasn't expecting anyone. Rebecca was in California; Jenna and Sheridan were in La Crosse; Sam was at the bookstore.

She opened the door.

Sheriff Martinez stood on the porch, hat in hand, expression solemn enough to make Hope's stomach drop.

"Mrs. Hawthorne," he said. "May I come in?"

Hope stepped aside, déjà vu washing over her. The last time he'd stood in this hallway, he'd told her Lily was dead. What could be worse than that?

"Is this about the driver?" Hope asked. "The trial?"

"It is." Martinez followed her to the living room and waited until she sat before continuing. "We've made an arrest. The driver who fled the scene was picked up in Trempealeau County after another DUI. He'll face charges for the crash and for fleeing the scene."

Hope's hands tightened on the armrest. "Good."

"There's more." Martinez pulled a clear evidence bag from his coat. "We recovered your daughter's belongings from the vehicle. Her purse. And her phone."

Hope stared at the bag. She could see Lily's phone case through the plastic—the one with pressed flowers Sheridan had made for her birthday. The screen was cracked, spider-webbed across the image of Hope and Lily at the state fair last summer.

"The phone's been processed as evidence," Martinez said gently. "Once the case is closed, you can claim it. Along with her other belongings. I wanted to let you know in person."

Hope couldn't speak. That phone had been in Lily's hand. Had been texting *Jenna's driving like someone's grandmother. We'll be there soon. Love you.* ✿

Had been mid-message when everything ended.

"I know this doesn't make it easier," Martinez continued. "But he's in custody now. He can't hurt anyone else. And you'll have her things back. When you're ready."

After Martinez left, Hope sat on the couch and stared at nothing.

She'd known, intellectually, that Lily's phone had been in the crash. That it had ended up somewhere. But hearing it confirmed—that it had been with the driver all this time, that she'd get it back eventually—made something shift in her chest.

A door closing. Not painfully. Just...finally.

The accident had happened. The driver had fled. The phone had been lost. And now the driver was caught, and the phone would be returned, and this chapter—the legal one, the justice one—was ending.

She pulled out her own phone and texted Sam: *The sheriff stopped by. They caught the driver. They have Lily's phone.*

Sam's reply came quickly: *Are you okay?*

Hope thought about it. Was she?

Hope: *I think so. It's strange. I thought I'd be angrier. But mostly I just feel... tired. Ready for this part to be over.*

That's allowed. You don't have to perform rage if you don't feel it.

Hope: *Rebecca would say I'm processing.*

Sam: *Rebecca would be right.*

Hope: *Do you still want to have coffee tomorrow? I understand if you need space.*

Sam: *I still want to. If you do.*

Hope: *I do. Ten a.m.? I'll meet you there.*

Sam: *See you then.*

Hope set her phone down and looked around the living room—at the manuscripts on the table, the coffee cup from this morning, the worn armchair where she and Lily used to read together.

She'd survived six months without Lily. Had learned to breathe around the grief. Had found Sam in the most impossible way.

And now this final piece—the driver, the phone, the concrete reminder of that night—was being put to rest.

That evening, Hope sat in Lily's room and pulled out the quote cards, shuffling through them like she sometimes did when she needed Lily's voice.

She drew one at random:

"The universe is made of stories, not of atoms." — *Muriel Rukeyser*

Hope smiled. Leave it to Lily to leave a quote about storytelling.

Maybe this was Lily's story, still unfolding. The girl tries to set up her mom. The girl dies. The universe steps in to finish what she started. Bookstore owner gets a wrong number. Responds anyway. Helps a grieving mother survive. Turns out to be the man the daughter had chosen.

It was either the universe's idea of poetry or the cruelest coincidence imaginable.

Hope chose to believe it was poetry.

She texted Sam: *Found one of Lily's quote cards. It says, "The universe is made of stories, not of atoms."*

Sam: *Muriel Rukeyser. That's a good one.*

Hope: *I think Lily would say this is part of her story— you and me, the texts, all of it.*

Sam: *What would she say about it?*

Hope: *Probably, "I told you you'd like each other," followed by seventeen smug emojis.*

Sam: *That sounds exactly right.*

Hope: *She was very pleased with herself when she plotted things.*

Sam: *She had good taste.*

Hope: *In bookstore owners?*

Sam: *In people.*

Hope set her phone down and looked around Lily's room at the unmade bed, the sticky notes on the mirror, the plants still reaching toward the window.

"Thank you," Hope whispered to the air. "For Sam. For the bookstore. For the texts that kept me alive. I don't know if you orchestrated this, but if you did… thank you."

The room didn't answer, but the house settled around her in a way that felt almost like agreement.

Hope took one of Lily's quote cards and tucked it into her wallet:

"Stories save lives." —Rebecca Solnit

Tomorrow she'd have coffee with Sam, not as strangers, not as text-message friends, but as two people trying to figure out what came next. She would have to get up early to get to LaCrosse.

Tomorrow she'd sit where Lily sat and drink what Lily drank, and tell Sam stories about the daughter who'd tried so hard to make them meet.

Tomorrow she'd keep living, keep surviving, keep taking steps forward even when the path was unclear.

Three inches to the left.

She was getting there.

SAM

Saturday morning, Sam opened the store early, just to keep his hands busy. He'd been nervous all week about today's meeting with Hope, in person, in public, at the place Lily had loved.

It felt significant, like they were crossing an invisible threshold from text friendship to real friendship.

Or maybe something more.

Sam didn't let himself think about that.

At 9:45 a.m., he locked up and walked the three blocks to the coffee shop. The Daily Grind was crowded with weekend regulars, but he found a small table by the window and waited.

Hope arrived at 9:58 a.m., two minutes early, looking nervous and beautiful in jeans and Lily's favorite sweater.

"Hi," she said.

"Hi," Sam said.

They smiled at each other like teenagers on a first date, awkward, earnest, and trying a little too hard.

"Should we get coffee?" Hope asked.

"Probably."

They ordered at the counter, black coffee for Sam, tea for Hope, and on impulse, Sam added two scones.

"You and your scones," Hope teased.

"They're comfort food."

"They're carbs and butter."

"That's what makes them comforting."

They sat at the table by the window. The scones sat between them like a peace offering.

"So," Hope said.

"So," Sam echoed.

"This is weird."

"Extremely weird."

"We talked for four hours on the phone Tuesday, and now I can't think of anything to say."

"Same," Sam admitted. "My brain's gone completely blank."

Hope laughed, and just like that, the tension eased.

They talked about the bookstore, about Hope's editing work, about the student who'd come in yesterday looking for "something to make me feel feelings but not too many feelings."

"What did you recommend?" Hope asked.

"The House in the Cerulean Sea," Sam said. "It makes you feel things, but they're mostly good ones."

"I love that book."

"Lily did too. She bought three copies, one to keep, one to give away, and one as backup in case she gave the first one away and wanted to reread it."

Hope smiled. "That's such a Lily thing to do."

"She was very generous with her books. I'd see her buying the same title multiple times. When I asked why, she said, 'I can't give someone a book I've already read. It needs to be fresh and have an unbroken spine. That first-read magic.'"

"She said the same thing about library books," Hope said. "Wouldn't borrow them because they'd been read too many times. Said they felt tired."

"Books as living things," Sam said. "She really believed that."

"She did."

They were quiet for a moment, resting in the comfort of shared memory.

"Can I ask you something?" Hope said.

"Anything."

"When did you know? That you wanted to help me? That you weren't just going to respond once and move on?"

Sam considered. "When you said, 'I don't know how to do this. How to be in the world when you're not in it.' That was the moment. Because I recognized that desperation, that need for someone, anyone, just to stay."

"Did someone stay for you? After Elise?"

"Not like that. I had friends who checked in, kind customers. But no one who just... sat with me in the dark. That part I had to do alone."

"I'm sorry."

"Don't be. It taught me how to help you. I knew what I'd needed but hadn't received, so I tried to give you that."

Hope reached across the table and covered his hand with hers just for a moment, long enough to say thank you without words.

They finished their coffee, ate their scones, and talked about everything and nothing.

"Want to see the bookstore?" Sam asked. "I know you've been, but I could show you around properly the sections Lily loved, the quote cards we've found."

I'd like that," Hope said.

They walked the three blocks side by side, not quite touching but close enough that their arms brushed occasionally.

At Turner's, Sam unlocked the door and let her in. The store was quiet, dim, perfect.

"This is my favorite time," Sam said. "Before it opens. When it's just me and the books."

"I can see why."

Sam showed her the poetry section where Lily had left the most quote cards, the fantasy shelves where she'd discovered new worlds, and the small table where she'd sat with other students during impromptu study groups.

"She made this place better," Sam said. "Just by being here."

"She had that effect," Hope agreed.

Upstairs, Hope sat in the leather chair by the window. Sam stood back and watched her, the way the light touched her face, the way her fingers traced the chair's arm, the way her gaze found the same view Lily once loved.

"I can see why she sat here," Hope said. "The light is perfect."

"Good light," Sam said.

Hope looked at him, really looked. "Thank you."

"For what?"

"For this. For showing me her world. For helping me understand who she was here, who she became."

"She was remarkable here," Sam said. "But she was remarkable because of you. You raised that."

Hope's eyes went bright. "I did my best."

"It was enough. More than enough."

They stayed at the bookstore for an hour. Sam showed her the first editions he was proud of. Hope shared stories from Lily's childhood. Together, they existed in that quiet space between grief and joy, between loss and connection, between what had been and what might still be.

When Hope finally left, Sam walked her to her car.

"Thank you for today," Hope said. "For coffee. For the bookstore. For making this easy."

"It was easy," Sam said. "Being with you is easy."

Hope smiled. "Even when I'm a mess?"

"You're not a mess. You're grieving. There's a difference."

"Sam?"

"Yes?"

"Would you want to do this again? Not texting. Not calling. Just… this. Being together."

Sam's heart did something tender and unexplainable. "Yes. I'd like that very much."

"Good." Hope got in her car. "I'll text you when I get home."

"Please do."

Sam watched her drive away, something warm and fragile blooming in his chest, something that felt a lot like hope.

He opened the store for the afternoon shift, helped students find books, recommended poetry to someone heartbroken, and found a cookbook for someone learning to cook for one.

And every time his phone buzzed with a message from Hope, he smiled.

That night, they talked on the phone for three hours.

"I think Lily would be pleased," Hope said.

"About what?"

"Us. Talking. Being friends."

"Is that what we are?" Sam asked. "Friends?"

Hope was quiet for a moment. "I think so. For now. Is that okay?"

"For now, it's perfect," Sam said.

And he meant it. or now, it was all they needed.

For now, it was enough.

THE NUMBER AFTER YOU

CHAPTER 10: The Weight of Quiet

Mid-June, five weeks after the revelation

HOPE

The Thursday afternoon call from Dr. Amy Danner shouldn't have surprised Hope, but it did.

"Ms. Hawthorne," Dr. Danner said warmly. "I hope I'm not catching you at a bad time."

Hope closed her laptop, abandoning the manuscript she'd been half-heartedly editing. "Not at all. What can I do for you?"

"I wanted to let you know the Book Rescue program launches next week. The shelf is installed in the student center, and we've been collecting books and quote cards. Some students have already started leaving notes for each other." Dr. Danner paused. "I thought you might like to attend the ribbon cutting if that's not too difficult."

Hope's throat tightened. Lily's project. The one she'd dreamed of but never got to see.

"I'd like that," Hope managed. "When?"

"Next Thursday at three. Nothing formal, just a small dedication. Sam Turner helped tremendously with the setup; he's been invaluable. I assume you two have stayed in touch?"

"We have," Hope said, smiling before she could stop herself. "He's... he's been a good friend."

"I'm glad. Lily would've liked that."

After they hung up, Hope immediately texted Sam: *Did you know about the Book Rescue launch next Thursday?*

His response came quickly: *Yes. Dr. Danner asked me to help set it up. I was going to tell you. Were you invited?*

Just now. Are you going?

I was planning to. Would you want to go together? I could pick you up and save you the drive.

Hope stared at the message. Sam is offering to drive two and a half hours to pick her up, then two and a half hours back to La Crosse, and then do it all again to bring her home.

That's a lot of driving for you, she typed.

I don't mind. I like getting to spend that time in your company.

Hope felt warmth spread through her chest. *I like your company too. Okay. Pick me up at noon?*

Sam: *I'll bring coffee.*

Hope: *You're perfect.*

She sent it before she could stop herself. Then stared at the words glowing on her screen.

You're perfect.

Three dots appeared. Disappeared. Appeared again.

Sam: *No one's ever called me perfect before.*

Hope: *First time for everything.*

Sam: *Hope?*

Hope's heart stumbled, then raced.

She typed: *Does that scare you?*

Sam: *Terrifies me. You?*

Hope: *Same.*

Sam: *Do we… talk about it? Or just let it be?*

Hope considered. They'd been circling this for weeks, the long phone calls, the late-night texts that made her smile, the way her stomach flipped when his name lit her screen. She'd even mentioned him to Rebecca, probably more than seventeen times by now.

Hope: *Let's see how Thursday goes,* she typed. *Then maybe we can talk about it.*

Okay. That's good. I can do that.

Sam?

Yes?

I'm glad it's you, the texts, the bookstore, all of it. I'm glad it's you.

I'm glad it's you, too.

Hope set her phone down and pressed both palms to her face. Her cheeks flushed; her heart raced. She felt like a teenager, which was ridiculous. She was forty-two. She'd been married. Had a daughter. Had lived through loss and learned to rebuild.

But sitting in her kitchen on a Thursday afternoon, texting the bookstore owner who made her laugh, understood her grief, and was willing to drive five hours just to see her, made her feel young again. New. Terrified, in the best possible way.

She called Rebecca.

"I think I'm falling for him," Hope said without preamble.

"I know," Rebecca replied.

"You know?"

"Hope you've been falling for him since the first text. You just didn't know it was him yet."

"That doesn't make sense."

"It makes perfect sense. You fell for his words first, then his kindness, then his honesty. Now you're just catching up emotionally to what's been happening for weeks."

Hope sank into a chair. "What if I'm not ready?"

"For what?"

"For this. For him. For feelings that aren't about Lily."

"Hope." Rebecca's voice softened. "Feelings about Sam aren't separate from Lily. He loved her too. He's part of her story. Letting him into your life isn't moving on from her; it's honoring what she wanted for you."

"She wanted us to meet."

"She did. And you did. And now you're falling for each other exactly like she hoped you would. That's not betrayal, Hope. That's beautiful."

Hope wiped her eyes. "When did you get so wise?"

"I've always been this wise. You just finally decided to listen."

They talked for another hour about Sam, about grief, about how moving forward isn't the same as moving on. About how loving someone new doesn't mean loving someone less.

When they hung up, Hope felt steadier. Still scared. But steadier.

She texted Sam: *What should I wear to a Book Rescue launch?*

Something that says 'my daughter was brilliant, and I'm proud.'

So... normal clothes?

Normal clothes work.

Hope smiled and went upstairs to Lily's room. Opened the closet. Found the sweater Lily had bought her, the one she'd worn to the bookstore that first visit.

"Is it okay?" Hope whispered to the quiet room. "To fall for him? To let this happen?"

The air stayed still, but the afternoon light through the window fell across Lily's desk, illuminating a sticky note she hadn't noticed before:

Remember, joy is a muscle.

Hope laughed through her tears. "Okay, baby. I'll try."

SAM

Thursday morning, Sam woke at five a.m., even though he didn't need to leave until nine-thirty.

He showered. Changed his shirt twice. Made coffee and forgot to drink it. Pacing his apartment, he only stopped when his neighbor knocked on the wall.

This wasn't just a drive to an event. It was five hours in a car with Hope, five hours of conversation, of silence, of proximity to a woman who made his heart do complicated things.

A woman who'd texted *You're perfect,* and *I'm glad it's you*, and made him believe that maybe, possibly, he could have this again, a connection, warmth, and someone who understood him.

At nine, Sam loaded the truck with coffee (good coffee, from the shop Hope liked), water bottles, and a bag of blueberry scones from Margaret's.

At nine-thirty, he pulled out of the parking lot and pointed the truck toward Hope's yellow Victorian, two and a half hours away.

The drive was familiar now. He'd made it a hundred times in his head, picturing her house, picturing her waiting on the porch.

Her neighborhood looked exactly as he'd imagined: tree-lined streets, old houses with character, the kind of place where people still waved to each other and left porch lights on for comfort.

The yellow Victorian sat on a corner lot, cheerful and lived-in, with a porch that seemed made for reading in good weather. Sam could picture Lily growing up here. Could picture Hope raising her here alone after the divorce.

He parked in the driveway and texted: *I'm here. No rush.*

The front door opened before he could get out.

Hope stood on the porch in jeans and Lily's sweater, hair loose around her shoulders, smiling like she'd been waiting by the window.

Sam's heart did that thing again, the complicated thing, the one that felt dangerously close to falling.

He got out of the truck, suddenly aware of every movement, every breath.

"Hi," Hope said.

"Hi," Sam replied.

They stood there for a moment, grinning at each other like fools.

"You brought coffee," Hope said, eyeing the cups in the console.

"And scones."

"You're perfect."

"You said that already."

"Doesn't make it less true."

Sam laughed, surprised at how easy it was to laugh around her. "Ready to go?

"Let me grab my bag."

Hope disappeared inside and returned with a small backpack. Sam held the passenger door for her, a gesture that felt old-fashioned and right.

"Such a gentleman," Hope teased.

"My mother would haunt me if I wasn't."

They settled into the truck. Sam handed Hope her drink, tea, not coffee, the kind she liked, and pulled out of the driveway.

For the first twenty minutes, they were quiet. Not awkward. Just… adjusting. Learning the rhythm of each other in this new space.

Then Hope said, "Tell me about your mother."

And just like that, they were talking.

Sam told her about his mother, who'd taught him to love books before he could read. About his father, who worked construction and read mystery novels on his lunch breaks. About growing up in a house where stories mattered more than money.

Hope told him about her parents, her mother, who'd died when Lily was five, and her father, who'd remarried, moved to Florida, and sent cards twice a year as if that were enough.

"Rebecca and I raised each other, really," Hope said. "After Mom died. Dad was there physically but not… present. We learned to be our own family."

"Is that why you're so close?"

"Trauma bonding," Hope said lightly. "The best kind of bonding."

They talked about David's divorce, the distance, and the way some people chose their own comfort over their children's needs.

"I'm sorry he did that," Sam said. "To you and to Lily."

"Me too. But it made us closer. Made her mine in a way she might not have been if he'd stayed."

"That's a generous way to look at it."

"It's the only way that doesn't make me bitter." Hope sipped her coffee. "What about you? Any ex-wives hiding in your past besides Elise?"

"Just one. College sweetheart. We got married too young and divorced three years later. Amicable. She lives in Oregon now with her husband and two kids. We still send Christmas cards."

"That's very civilized."

"We were better as friends than as spouses."

"And Elise?"

"She was everything," Sam said simply. "The right person at the right time. We had eight years together. Not enough, but I'm grateful for them."

Hope reached over and squeezed his hand. Just once. Long enough to say without words: I understand.

They stopped for gas about an hour in. Hope got out and stretched, arching her back like a cat.

"I forgot how long this drive is," she said.

"We're halfway."

"Want me to drive the rest?" she asked.

"I'm good. But thank you."

At the mini-mart, they wandered the aisles like tourists reading ridiculous magazine headlines, judging snack options, laughing at absolutely nothing important.

"We should get beef jerky," Hope said.

"Why?"

"Road trips require beef jerky. It's the law."

"Is it?"

"I'm pretty sure Lily told me that once."

Sam bought the beef jerky. And chips. And chocolate. And a bottle of water shaped like a penguin because Hope said it was cute.

Back in the truck, they ate junk food and talked about books, the ones that had changed them, the authors they'd follow anywhere, the stories they'd reread until the spines cracked.

"If you could only reread one book for the rest of your life," Hope said, "what would it be?"

Sam thought for a moment. *"The Night Circus.* Elise's favorite. I read it every year on her birthday."

"That's beautiful."

"What about you?"

"A Tree Grows in Brooklyn. It got me through being pregnant and alone. It taught me you could survive poverty and heartbreak and still grow toward the light."

"That's who you are," Sam said. "Someone who grows toward the light."

Hope looked at him. "So are you."

They were quiet after that. The easy kind of quiet, the kind that means everything's been said.

About a half-hour from La Crosse, Hope said softly, "I'm nervous."

"About the Book Rescue launch?"

"About seeing Lily's project come to life without her. About standing in a room full of people who loved her and knowing she's not there to see it."

"She sees it," Sam said.

"You believe that?"

"I don't know what I believe. But I know this: when we build something in someone's name, it becomes part of them. She'll be in every book on that shelf, every note left for the next reader, every life saved by the right words at the right time."

Hope wiped her eyes. "You should've been a poet."

"I sell poetry. Close enough."

They pulled into La Crosse at 2:45, fifteen minutes to spare.

The campus was beautiful in June, lush and alive, students from summer classes sprawled on the lawns, the Mississippi River glinting beyond the buildings.

Sam parked near the student center, turned off the truck, and looked at Hope.

"Ready?" he asked.

"No. But I'm doing it anyway."

They walked into the building together. Not holding hands, but close enough that their shoulders brushed.

The Book Rescue shelf stood in the main lobby, impossible to miss, a handcrafted wooden display with a sign that read:

THE LILY HAWTHORNE BOOK RESCUE

Take what you need. Leave what you can. Pass it forward.

The shelf was already full of books, some new, some worn, all tagged with colored tabs. Tucked inside each one was a quote card: some in Lily's handwriting, others in her classmates.' All followed her familiar template:

For when you need [specific thing]. Try this.

Hope stopped in front of the display, a hand covering her mouth.

"It's perfect," she whispered.

Dr. Danner appeared beside her. "Ms. Hawthorne, I'm so glad you came."

"Thank you for doing this to make her dream real."

"We had help." Dr. Danner smiled at Sam. "He provided most of the books, and the students have been contributing all week. We already have fifty titles and more coming in."

A small crowd had gathered: students, faculty, a few local reporters. Someone handed Hope a pair of ceremonial scissors.

"Would you like to cut the ribbon?" Dr. Danner asked.

Hope looked at Sam. He nodded encouragement.

She stepped forward, scissors trembling slightly in her hand. The ribbon was purple, Lily's favorite color.

"My daughter believed stories could save lives," Hope said, her voice shaking but strong. "She spent months planning this, choosing books, writing notes, creating a space where people could find exactly what they needed, exactly when they needed it." She looked at the shelf. "She won't see this, but you will. And I hope, when you take a book from here, you think of her. Think of the girl who wanted to save you."

She cut the ribbon.

Applause filled the room. Students crowded the shelf, browsing, exclaiming over titles, and reading quote cards aloud.

Hope watched them through tears, her face softened by something like peace.

Sam stood beside her close, but not touching, letting her have the moment.

After a while, a student approached, young and nervous, clutching a worn paperback.

"Ms. Hawthorne? I'm Emma. I knew Lily. She used to leave quote cards in my history textbook. They helped me survive finals."

She held out the book. "I wanted to contribute this. It helped me. Maybe it'll help someone else."

Hope took *The Perks of Being* a Wallflower and opened it. Inside was a quote card in Emma's handwriting:

For when you feel like you don't belong anywhere. You do. I promise.

"Thank you," Hope whispered.

"No, thank you. For raising someone who cared about strangers."

Emma walked away. Hope pressed the book to her chest.

"Okay?" Sam asked quietly.

"More than okay."

They stayed for an hour. Hope spoke with students who'd known Lily, who'd found her notes, whose words had been saved.

Sam hung back, watching Hope light up as one story after another revealed how deeply her daughter had mattered.

Before they left, Hope added a book to the shelf: *A Tree Grows in Brooklyn*. Inside, a quote card in her own handwriting read: *For when you're surviving something impossible. You're stronger than you know. Keep growing toward the light.*

The sun was setting as they walked back to Sam's truck. Hope realized she hadn't booked a hotel yet—she'd been so focused on the Book Rescue launch that she hadn't thought past it.

"There's a hotel about two blocks from the bookstore," Sam said, as if reading her mind. "Nothing fancy, but clean. Good breakfast."

"That sounds perfect."

Sam drove her there, carried her overnight bag to the lobby, and lingered by the front desk like he didn't want to leave.

"Thank you for today," Hope said. "For being there. For helping make it real."

"Thank you for letting me be part of it."

They stood in the hotel lobby, neither quite ready to say goodbye.

"Hope?"

"Yes?"

"Would you want to have dinner with me tomorrow night? A real dinner. Not just coffee or a memorial. An actual date."

Hope's heart did something complicated and warm. "Yes. I'd like that very much."

"I could pick you up here. Around six?"

"Six is perfect."

Sam smiled, that soft smile that made her chest tighten. "It's a date then."

He started to leave, then turned back. "Hope?"

"Yes?"

"I'm really glad you're staying. That I get to see you tomorrow."

"Me too."

After he left, Hope checked into her room and immediately called Rebecca.

"I'm having dinner with him tomorrow," Hope said. "An actual date. Not a coffee date. A real date."

"Finally," Rebecca said. "I was wondering when you two would stop pretending this was just friendship."

"We weren't pretending."

"Hope, you've been in love with him for weeks. You just didn't know it was him yet."

Hope sank onto the hotel bed. "What if I'm not ready?"

"For what?"

"For this. For him. For feelings that aren't about Lily."

"Hope," Rebecca said gently. "Feelings about Sam aren't separate from Lily. He loved her too. He's part of her story. Letting him into your life isn't moving on from her—it's honoring what she wanted for you."

After they hung up, Hope lay in the unfamiliar hotel bed and texted Sam: *Thank you for today. For the Book Rescue. For asking me to dinner. For all of it.*

Sam: *Thank you for saying yes. Get some rest. Big day tomorrow.*

Hope: *Big day?*

Sam: *Our first official date. That's big.*

Hope smiled at her phone. *It is big. Terrifying, actually.*

Sam: *Good terrifying or bad terrifying?*

Hope: *Good terrifying. The kind that means something matters.*

Sam: *You matter. This matters. Sleep well, Hope.*

Hope: *Goodnight, Sam.*

She fell asleep with her phone on the nightstand and a smile on her face, thinking about bookstores and second chances, and daughters who still found ways to orchestrate love from beyond.

CHAPTER 11: Saying the Quiet Thing

The First Date

HOPE

Hope woke in the hotel room to sunlight streaming through unfamiliar curtains and a moment of disorientation before remembering: La Crosse. Book Rescue. Tonight. Sam.

She had twelve hours to prepare for a date, which was either way too much time or nowhere near enough.

She texted Rebecca: *I don't know what to wear. Do I own date clothes? What are date clothes?*

Rebecca: *Deep breaths. You're adorable. Wear the navy dress. The one Lily picked out.*

Hope: *That feels significant.*

Rebecca: *It is significant. That's the point.*

Hope spent the morning walking around La Crosse, partly to kill time, partly to see Lily's world. She found the coffee shop the girls had loved, ordered Lily's usual (iced mocha with extra whipped cream), and sat by the window watching students pass by.

She wondered how many of them had found Lily's quote cards. How many lives her daughter had touched without knowing.

At noon, she texted Sam: *What kind of restaurant are we going to? I need to know how fancy to get.*

Sam: *Nothing fancy. Just good food, good wine, good company. You could wear pajamas and it would be perfect.*

Hope: *I'm not wearing pajamas on our first date.*

Sam: *Fair enough. Whatever you wear will be perfect then.*

Hope: *You're very smooth for a bookstore owner.*

Sam: *I've been practicing in the mirror. It's been going well.*

Jenna and Sheridan were home for summer break so after lunch, Hope took a ride-share up to Grandad Bluff. It was the place she'd seen in that photo from Lily's memorial slideshow— her daughter with wind in her hair, looking out at the river like she was memorizing the view.

The driver, a chatty college student, told her it was where everyone went to think, to breathe, to remember why they'd chosen this town.

At the overlook, Hope stood where Lily had stood and looked out at the same sweeping view of the Mississippi, the three states meeting at the confluence, the town spread below like a map of her daughter's college years.

The wind was strong enough to steal her breath, and for a moment, Hope felt Lily's presence so clearly it made her chest ache. This was where Lily had come to see the big picture, to put her small worries into perspective.

Hope took a photo—not for posting, just for keeping—and whispered to the wind, "I see why you loved it here, baby. I understand now." The ride-share back down felt like a gentle descent from a sacred space, and Hope felt steadier somehow, ready for whatever the evening would bring.

Back at the hotel, Hope showered, blow-dried her hair, and changed outfits four times before admitting to herself that she was nervous.

Not first-date-in-high-school nervous. Not even first-date-after-divorce nervous.

This was different. *I'm falling for someone who knew my daughter, and this matters in ways I don't fully understand yet* nervous.

She finally settled on the navy dress Lily had helped her pick out two years ago—simple, elegant, the one Lily had said made her look "like a person who has their life together, even when you don't."

Hope stared at her reflection. "Is this okay?" she asked the empty room. Asked Lily, wherever she was. "Am I allowed to be this happy?"

Through the window, she could see the Mississippi River in the distance, the same river Lily had looked at from campus, had walked beside with her friends.

Hope chose to take it as a yes.

At exactly six p.m., her phone buzzed.

Sam: *I'm in the lobby. No rush. Take your time.*

Hope grabbed her purse, touched the quote card she'd tucked inside ("Stories save lives"), and headed downstairs.

Sam stood by the front desk in dark jeans and a button-down, holding flowers—daisies and wildflowers, nothing fancy, just the kind of bouquet that said *I thought about you* instead of *I'm trying to impress you.*

"Hi," Hope said.

"Hi," Sam echoed. Then, taking her in, "You look beautiful."

"You clean up pretty well yourself."

Sam handed her the flowers. "I didn't know if the hotel room had a vase, but I wanted you to have these anyway."

"They're perfect." Hope pressed her face to them, breathing in. "The desk can probably find something. Give me two minutes?"

The clerk found a small vase, and Hope arranged the flowers quickly, setting them on the desk in her room where she'd see them later.

When she came back down, Sam was waiting by the door.

"Ready?" he asked.

"Where are we going?"

"Do you trust me?"

Hope considered. Did she? Trust this man who'd helped her survive her worst weeks? Who'd built a memorial for her daughter? Who stood in a hotel lobby looking hopeful and maybe just as nervous as she was?

"Yes," Hope said. "I trust you."

SAM

Sam drove them to a restaurant Hope might have walked past a dozen times without noticing—tucked away on a side street in downtown La Crosse, the kind of place locals knew but tourists missed. Small, intimate, with fairy lights strung across a patio overlooking the river.

"How did you find this?" Hope asked as they settled at a table outside.

"Lily told me about it. Said she came here once with Jenna and Sheridan for Jenna's birthday. Said the food was good, and the view was better." Sam smiled. "I saved the recommendation. Thought maybe someday I'd bring someone here."

"And here we are."

"Here we are."

They ordered wine. Hope chose the pasta Lily had once raved about; Sam picked the fish the waiter recommended. And then they just... talked.

Not about grief. Not about Lily. Not about Elise.

About everything else.

Hope told him about her editing work, the authors she loved, the manuscripts that made her cry, the Oxford comma debate that nearly ended a friendship.

Sam told her about the bookstore, the regulars who'd become friends, the student who'd proposed to his girlfriend in the poetry section last spring.

"That's so romantic," Hope said.

"It was. They read each other poems instead of vows. There wasn't a dry eye in the store."

"Do you ever think about getting a bookstore cat?" Hope asked. "I feel like every good bookstore should have a cat."

Sam laughed. "I've thought about it. There's an orange tabby that keeps showing up at the back door. I've been feeding him. At this rate, he might just move in and make the decision for me."

"What would you name him?"

"Probably something literary. Dante. Or Atticus. Or just 'Cat' because I'm not creative with names."

Hope smiled. "I vote for Dante. It fits a bookstore."

They talked about travel—places they'd been, places they wanted to go. Hope confessed she'd barely left Wisconsin. Sam admitted he'd traveled widely with Elise but hadn't left the state since she died.

"It felt wrong," Sam said. "Seeing places without her. Experiencing things she'd wanted to see."

"Do you think you could now? Travel, I mean?"

Sam looked at Hope across the table, candlelight reflected in his eyes. "I think I could. With the right person."

The food arrived, and it was excellent. They shared bites, compared notes, and debated playfully whether the pasta or the fish was better.

"The pasta," Hope insisted.

"You're biased because Lily liked it."

"I'm biased because it's objectively superior."

"Objectively?" Sam laughed. "There's no objectivity in food preferences."

"Sure, there is. My opinion is the objective truth. Everything else is an error."

Sam grinned. "I can see where Lily got her confidence."

After dinner, they walked along the river. The path was lincd with old-fashioned lampposts that made everything feel like a scene from one of Hope's favorite novels.

"This is nice," Hope said softly.

"Which part?"

"All of it. Being here. With you. Not talking about grief for once."

"We can talk about grief if you want," Sam offered.

"I don't want. I want to talk about normal things. First-date things. Like... favorite movies. Or conspiracy theories. Or why you really keep a bookstore open when Amazon exists."

"Because Amazon doesn't have Dante."

"That's your only reason?"

Sam stopped walking and turned to face her.

"Because a bookstore is a place where people come to find things they didn't know they were looking for. Because sometimes someone walks in sad and leaves with a book that changes everything. Because Lily was right, stories save lives. And I want to be part of that."

Hope's eyes stung. "That's the most romantic thing anyone's ever said, and it wasn't even about me."

"Want me to say something romantic about you?"

"Maybe."

Sam took her hand properly this time, fingers laced, not just the casual touch from the truck.

"Hope Hawthorne," he said seriously. "You walked into my store five weeks ago, and my world tilted. You're brilliant and brave and funny and kind. You raised a daughter who changed my life, and now you're changing it again. And I know we're supposed to go slow, but I need you to know: this isn't grief seeking comfort. This is me falling for you. Really falling."

Hope couldn't speak. Could only stand there on that riverside path, her hand in his, her heart doing complicated things.

"Your turn," Sam said, suddenly nervous. "You can say something back. Or not. No pressure."

"Sam Turner," Hope said, finding her voice. "You texted me back when you didn't have to. You helped me survive when I didn't think I could. You built a memorial for my daughter with your own hands. And you make me laugh, which shouldn't be possible, but somehow is." She squeezed his hand. "I'm falling too. Really falling."

They stood there, smiling at each other like fools while other couples passed by and the river kept flowing and the world kept turning.

"Can I kiss you?" Sam asked.

"Please."

He did.

It was soft and tentative and sweet, the kind of first kiss that asks *Is this okay?* And answers yes, *this is okay*, and promises *there will be more.*

When they pulled apart, Hope was smiling so wide her face hurt.

"That was nice," she said.

"Just nice?"

"Fine. It was perfect. But I'm not inflating your ego on the first date."

"Second kiss?" Sam asked hopefully.

"Maybe second date."

"When's the second date?"

"Presumptuous, aren't we?"

"Hopeful," Sam corrected.

They walked back to the truck hand in hand. Sam drove through the quiet streets of La Crosse, one hand on the wheel and the other holding hers.

At the hotel, he walked her to the lobby entrance and paused.

"Thank you for tonight," Hope said.

"Thank you for giving me a chance."

They lingered in the amber glow of the hotel lights, neither wanting the night to end.

"Sam?"

"Yes?"

"I'm glad it's you."

"Me too."

He kissed her again—slower this time, deeper, the kind of kiss that said *I meant everything I said tonight* and *I'm not going anywhere*.

When they pulled apart, Hope was smiling so wide her face hurt.

"Good night," she said.

"Good night, Hope." Sam squeezed her hand once more. "Drive safe tomorrow. Text me when you get home?"

"I will."

"And Hope?"

"Yes?"

"Thank you for tonight. For everything."

Hope watched him walk back to his truck, then rode the elevator to her room in a quiet daze.

Inside, she leaned against the door with her hand over her heart. The flowers he'd brought sat on the desk, cheerful in their makeshift vase.

She pulled out her phone and texted Rebecca: *I kissed him. Twice. I think I'm in love.*

Rebecca: *I'm so excited for you! I've known for weeks. Welcome to the party.*

Hope: *How did you know?*

Rebecca: *Because you stopped asking permission to be happy. You just were.*

Hope read that three times. Let it settle.

She sat on the edge of the hotel bed, looking at the flowers, at her reflection in the dark window, at the city lights of La Crosse spread below.

She thought about Lily—how she'd walked these streets, studied in that bookstore, left quote cards in books for strangers to find. How she'd tried so hard to set her mother up with Sam, had talked about him constantly, had believed they'd be perfect for each other.

"I know you're probably laughing," Hope said to the quiet room. "Saying 'I told you so.' And you're right. He's perfect. Thank you for Sam. For the bookstore. For trying to set us up. I wish you were here to see it. But I think... I think maybe you are."

The room stayed quiet, but Hope felt lighter somehow, like she'd been given permission she didn't know she needed.

She changed into pajamas, washed her face, and climbed into the unfamiliar hotel bed.

Her phone buzzed.

Sam: *I just told my sister about you. She says I'm in love with you and that I shouldn't screw it up.*

Hope: *Wise woman.*

Sam: *Are you still awake?*

Hope: *Can't sleep. Too happy. Too scared. Too everything.*

Sam: *Same.*

Hope: *What are we doing, Sam?*

Sam: *I think we're falling in love. Slowly. Carefully. Like two people who've been hurt and are trying not to hurt each other.*

Hope: *That's exactly what we're doing.*

Sam: *Is that okay?*

Hope: *It's perfect.*

They texted for another hour about nothing, about everything, until Hope's responses slowed and Sam realized she was falling asleep.

Sam: *Go to sleep. I'll text you tomorrow.*

Hope: *Promise?*

Sam: *Promise. Sweet dreams, Hope.*

Hope: *Sweet dreams, Sam. Thank you for tonight.*

She set her phone on the nightstand and closed her eyes, thinking about bookstores and second chances, about daughters who still found ways to orchestrate love from beyond, about kisses by the river and hands held across console compartments.

Thinking about how grief could transform into something else—not gone, just moved three inches to the left, making room for joy to exist alongside it.

She fell asleep smiling, wrapped in hotel sheets that smelled like lavender detergent, dreaming of good light and better tomorrows.

SAM

Sam drove home going exactly the speed limit, hands steady at ten and two, wearing the biggest smile of his life.

He'd kissed Hope Hawthorne.

Twice.

And she'd kissed him back.

And she'd said she was falling too.

At his apartment, he immediately called his sister, Marie, who lived in Boston and who he hadn't spoken to in three months because he was terrible at staying in touch.

"Sam?" Marie answered, alarmed. "Is everything okay?"

"I went on a date."

Silence.

"Marie? Did you hear me?"

"I heard you. I'm just processing. You went on a date. An actual date. With a living human who's not a book."

"Her name's Hope. She's amazing. And I think I'm in love with her."

More silence. Then: "Oh my God. Tell me everything."

Sam told her. About the wrong number. The texts. Lily. The bookstore. The memorial. Book Rescue. All of it.

When he finished, Marie was crying.

"Elise would have loved her," Marie said.

"I think so too."

"And this girl, Lily, she tried to set you up before she died?"

"That's what her friends said."

"That's the most romantic thing I've ever heard. It's like she was your matchmaker from beyond."

"Hope said the same thing."

"Because it's true. Sam, this is huge. You haven't dated anyone since Elise. You barely left the apartment the first year. And now you're in love?"

"I think so."

"You think so? Or you know so?"

Sam thought about Hope's smile. Her laugh. The way she said his name. The way her hand felt in his. The way his chest tightened every time his phone buzzed with her name.

"I know so," he said.

"Then don't screw it up."

"Thanks for the vote of confidence."

"I mean it. You deserve this. You deserve to be happy again. Just... don't be stupid."

"Define stupid."

"Don't hide things. Don't pull away when you get scared. Don't assume she can read your mind. Communicate. Be honest. All the things you're bad at."

"Gee, thanks."

"I love you. That's why I'm telling you."

After they hung up, Sam sat in the dark, thinking about honesty. About communication. About all the ways he'd failed those things with Hope at the beginning.

He pulled out his phone.

Sam: *I just told my sister about you. She says I'm in love with you and that I shouldn't screw it up.*

They texted for another hour about nothing, about everything, until Hope's responses slowed and Sam realized she was falling asleep.

Sam: *Go to sleep. I'll text you tomorrow.*

Hope: *Promise?*

Sam: *Promise. Sweet dreams, Hope.*

Hope: *Sweet dreams, Sam. Thank you for tonight.*

Sam set his phone on the nightstand and lay in the dark, thinking about bookstores and grieving mothers, and daughters who still managed to save people even after they were gone.

Thinking about second chances, first kisses, and the possibility that maybe loss wasn't the end of the story, just the middle.

EPILOGUE: Good Light

Christmas Eve

The yellow Victorian looked exactly the same.

Hope pulled into the driveway and sat for a moment, engine idling, taking it in. The porch where she'd waited for Lily to come home from college. The window of Lily's room, still holding the same curtains, the same light.

Six months since she'd moved to La Crosse, into the apartment above Turner's Books. Six months of living with Sam, working at the table by the window, feeding Dante at ungodly hours, falling asleep to the sound of the city instead of this quiet street.

But the house hadn't changed. She'd kept it exactly as it was. A museum, Sam called it. A love letter, Hope thought. A place to return to when she needed to remember who she'd been, who Lily had been, who they'd been together.

"You okay?" Sam asked from the passenger seat.

"Yeah." Hope turned off the engine. "It's just strange. Being back."

"We don't have to stay here. We could get a hotel."

"No. I want to be here. With Rebecca. With you. In Lily's house." Hope smiled. "It's just . . . I'm not the same person who lived here. I don't know if I fit anymore."

"You fit everywhere you decide to fit," Sam said, taking her hand. "That's what I've learned from you."

The front door flew open, and not just Rebecca burst onto the porch.

Jenna and Sheridan flanked her, all three of them grinning like they'd been plotting something.

"You're here!" Rebecca called. "Finally!"

"We've been watching out the window like creeps," Jenna added. "Sheridan's been doing commentary. 'They're parking. Now they're talking. Now they're just sitting there. Are they ever getting out?'"

"I was providing valuable intel," Sheridan protested.

Hope laughed and got out of the car. Rebecca pulled her into a fierce hug first, then Jenna, then Sheridan, until Hope was wrapped in a tangle of arms and love.

"What are you two doing here?" Hope asked, delighted.

"Rebecca invited us," Jenna said. "Said it was a 'family Christmas' and we're family."

"Also, she bribed us with cookies," Sheridan added.

"So many cookies," Jenna confirmed.

Sam came around the car with their bags, and Jenna immediately went in for a hug.

"Sam! Our favorite bookstore owner! How's Dante?"

"Judgmental and orange," Sam said. "Same as always."

"Perfect. Consistency is important in cats." Jenna turned to Hope. "Did you know Sam sends us pictures of Dante? Like, all the time?"

"I did not know that."

"It's true," Sheridan said, showing Hope her phone. "Look. This is from Tuesday. He's sitting on a stack of books looking deeply offended."

"He knocked them over five seconds later," Sam admitted.

Rebecca ushered them all inside. "Come on, it's freezing. I made cookies. Too many cookies. We're going to be sick of cookies by tomorrow."

The house smelled like cinnamon and vanilla and home. Rebecca had put up a small tree in the living room, decorated with ornaments Hope and Lily had made over the years. Construction paper snowflakes from elementary school, painted pine cones, a Star Wars ornament Lily had insisted on when she was eight because "the Force is strong with Christmas."

"I couldn't help myself," Rebecca said, seeing Hope's expression. "I wanted it to feel like she's still here."

"She is still here," Hope said softly.

"Obviously," Jenna said. "She's probably watching right now, taking notes on how we're decorating without her."

"She'd have opinions," Sheridan agreed. "Strong opinions about ornament placement."

"She once moved every ornament on our apartment tree because she said they weren't 'balanced,'" Jenna said. "Took her two hours. Then Sheridan bumped it and half of them fell off."

"That was an accident!"

"You hip-checked the tree, Sheridan."

"I was dancing! The music was very compelling!"

Sam laughed, and Hope watched him relax into the chaos, into the warmth of being with people who understood, who loved Lily, who were becoming his family too.

They spent the afternoon in the kitchen, making Christmas Eve dinner together. The same meal Hope and Lily had made every year. Lily wasn't there to make dinner with her, but she was trying to enjoy the day with the girls.

Jenna told stories about her studies and classmates. Sheridan talked about student teaching ("Turns out, middle-schoolers are terrifying. They can smell fear."). Rebecca shared carefully anonymized therapy stories. Sam described the bookstore's holiday rush and Dante's increasing territorial behavior.

"He sat in the window yesterday and hissed at every customer," Sam said. "Like he was personally offended by people wanting to buy books."

"That's because he is personally offended," Hope said. "He thinks the books are his."

"Technically, he's not wrong," Sam conceded.

After dinner, Rebecca insisted on cleaning up. "You four go relax. I've got this."

"She's plotting something," Hope whispered as they moved to the living room.

"Definitely plotting," Jenna agreed. "She's had that look all day."

"What look?" Sheridan asked.

"The 'I know something you don't know' look."

They settled in the living room with mugs of hot chocolate. Jenna immediately claimed the best spot on the couch. Sheridan stole a throw blanket. Sam sat beside Hope, their hands linked, while they talked about nothing and everything.

"Can we go up to Lily's room?" Jenna asked after a while. "I haven't seen it since . . . since we were here for the funeral."

"Of course," Hope said.

They climbed the stairs together, all four of them. At the top, Hope paused outside Lily's door.

"Ready?" she asked.

"Ready," they said in unison.

Hope opened the door.

The room was exactly as Lily had left it. The unmade bed. The textbooks on the desk. The sticky notes on the mirror, some from Lily, some Hope had added:

Joy is a muscle

You are allowed to be here

Thank you for Sam

I hope you're proud

Jenna walked straight to the bed and sat down, pulling Lily's quilt around her shoulders. Sheridan joined her, and they sat there looking around the room with the kind of quiet reverence that comes from missing someone.

"It smells like her," Sheridan said softly. "Her shampoo."

"I keep buying it," Hope admitted. "I may rub a little on her pillow sometimes."

"That's a little weird," Jenna said.

"That's love, " Sheridan said.

Sam walked slowly around the room, taking it in. He paused at the desk, at the wooden quote box, at the wall of photos documenting Lily's life.

"This is where she grew up," he said softly.

"This is where we both grew up," Hope corrected. "After David left, it was just us. This room, this house . . . it was our whole world for a long time."

"She was so happy here," Jenna said. "She'd come back from weekends home and tell us stories. About cooking with you, about movie marathons, about how you'd stay up too late talking about books."

"She said you were her best friend," Sheridan added. "Not in a weird, codependent way. Just . . . in a true way."

Hope's throat tightened. "She was mine too."

"Can I look at the quote box?" Sam asked.

"Of course."

He opened the wooden box on Lily's desk. Hope had gone through it a hundred times. Read every card. But watching Sam carefully move through them, reading Lily's handwriting, touching the index cards she'd touched, made Hope's chest ache in the best way.

"She had such careful handwriting," Sam said. "Every letter perfect."

"She used to practice," Hope said. "In middle school. She'd write the same quote over and over until it looked exactly how she wanted."

At the very bottom of the box, beneath all the familiar cards, Sam paused.

"Hope," he said quietly. "There's one more."

"What?"

He pulled out a card Hope had somehow never seen. Not a quote from someone famous.

Just three words in Lily's looping script:

P.S. Say yes.

Jenna sat up straight. "What does it say?"

Sam showed them the card.

Sheridan gasped. Jenna's eyes went wide.

"Oh my God," Jenna whispered. "She planned this. She actually planned this."

"That's so Lily," Sheridan said, starting to cry. "Leaving instructions."

Hope just stared at the card, unable to speak.

Sam took her hand, the quote card still in his other palm.

"I had a whole speech planned," Sam said, his voice rough. "Wrote it down, but I forgot it."

"But standing here in Lily's room, with her telling you to say yes, and the girls and Rebecca, who I think is definitely listening from the hallway . . . "

"I am!" Rebecca called from outside the door.

Everyone laughed through their tears.

"I think I can skip the speech," Sam continued, "and just ask."

He pulled a small box from his pocket with one hand, still holding Hope's hand with the other. Velvet, dark blue, worn at the edges like it had been carried for a while.

Jenna grabbed Sheridan's hand. Both of them were crying now.

"Hope Hawthorne," Sam said, his voice steady but his hands shaking. "You texted me on the worst day of your life, and I texted back, and somehow we built something beautiful from all that grief. You made me believe I could be happy again. Made me believe love wasn't finished with me." His eyes went bright. "I want to spend the rest of my life making you happy. Living above the bookstore with you and that judgmental cat. Helping students find the right books. Keeping Lily's memory alive. Growing old together. Growing toward the light together."

He opened the box. Inside was a simple gold band with a small diamond. Nothing flashy, just beautiful.

"Will you marry me?"

Hope looked at Sam, at the ring, at Lily's card, at Jenna and Sheridan crying on the bed, at Rebecca now openly standing in the doorway wiping her eyes.

"Yes," Hope whispered. Then louder: "Yes. Yes, of course yes."

Sam slid the ring onto her finger, and it fit perfectly. Like it had been waiting for her all along.

They kissed in Lily's room, surrounded by her two best friends, her aunt, her sticky notes and books and photos and memories, while outside the window snow began to fall in soft, quiet flakes.

When they pulled apart, everyone was crying.

"She planned this," Hope said, holding up the card. "She actually left instructions for our engagement."

"That's the most Lily thing ever," Jenna said, laughing through tears. "She couldn't let you do it without her approval."

"She's probably so smug right now," Sheridan added.

"She is," Rebecca said from the doorway. "Wherever she is, she's absolutely insufferable about being right."

They all laughed, and it felt good to laugh in Lily's room, to fill it with joy instead of just grief.

"Group hug," Jenna declared. "Everyone. Now."

They crowded together in the middle of Lily's room, all five of them, arms around each other, crying and laughing and celebrating.

"She'd love this," Hope said. "She'd love that you're all here. That we're all together."

"We'll always be together," Sheridan said. "That's what she wanted."

They spent the rest of the evening downstairs, calling people, showing off the ring, eating too many cookies. Jenna told the story of the proposal three different times, each version more embellished than the last.

"And then the snow started falling," Jenna said dramatically to someone on speakerphone. "Like the universe was blessing the moment."

"It was already snowing," Sheridan corrected.

"You're ruining my narrative."

Later, after Jenna and Sheridan had left, and Rebecca had finally gone to bed ("I'm giving you two some privacy, but I'm very happy, and we're discussing wedding details tomorrow"), Hope and Sam sat on the couch in the dark, watching the tree lights blink.

"Can I ask you something?" Hope said.

"Anything."

"When did you buy the ring?"

"Two months ago. I've been carrying it around, waiting for the right moment."

"And tonight was the right moment?"

"Lily's card made it the right moment. 'Say yes' felt like permission. Like she was giving us her blessing."

Hope leaned her head on his shoulder. "Do you think she knows? Wherever she is?"

"I think she orchestrated the whole thing. From the reassigned phone number to the quote card to the proposal. I think she's been stage-managing our love story from the beginning."

"That sounds like her."

They sat in comfortable silence, watching the snow fall outside the window, covering the yellow Victorian in white.

"Sam?"

"Hm?"

"Thank you for texting me back. That first day. When you didn't have to."

"Thank you for not blocking me when you found out who I was."

"Thank you for being exactly who Lily hoped you'd be."

"Thank you for letting me love you."

Hope kissed him softly. Then she pulled back and smiled. "We should check on Dante tomorrow. Margaret's probably spoiling him."

"Definitely spoiling him. She sends me updates. Last one said, 'He's eaten three times today and is very pleased with himself.'"

"That's our cat."

"Our cat," Sam repeated, smiling. "I like the sound of that."

They sat there a while longer, not ready to move, just existing in the warmth of being together, of being engaged, of being exactly where they were supposed to be.

Finally, Hope stood and held out her hand. "Come on. Let's go to bed. Tomorrow Rebecca's going to wake us up at dawn demanding wedding details."

"Probably."

They climbed the stairs together. At the top, Hope paused outside Lily's door one more time.

"Good night, baby," she whispered. "Thank you for saying yes for me."

In her old room, Hope changed into pajamas and climbed into the bed that used to be hers. Sam joined her, and they lay in the dark, listening to the house settle, to the quiet sounds of the place where everything had begun.

"Hope?" Sam said softly.

"Mm?"

"I'm really glad you texted that wrong number."

Hope smiled in the darkness. "Me too."

She held up her hand, watching the ring catch the moonlight through the window. The same moonlight that had fallen on this house for all the years she'd raised Lily here. The same light that now fell on her new life, her new love, her new beginning.

But not an ending. Never an ending.

Just a transformation.

"I love you," Hope whispered.

"I love you too."

They fell asleep like that. Engaged, happy, held by the house where everything had started and everything had changed.

In the morning, when Hope woke to Christmas Day, she went downstairs to find Rebecca already making coffee, humming to herself.

"Morning," Rebecca said, smiling. "How's my newly engaged sister?"

"Happy," Hope said simply. "Really, really happy."

"Good." Rebecca handed her a mug. "That's all I ever wanted for you."

They sat at the kitchen table, the same table where Hope had eaten breakfast with Lily for twenty years, and talked about wedding plans, about life, about how strange and beautiful it was that grief could transform into something else.

"She'd be proud of you," Rebecca said. "Of how you survived this. Of how you learned to live again."

"I couldn't have done it without you. Without Sam. Without Jenna and Sheridan. Without everyone who stayed."

"That's how it works," Rebecca said. "We hold each other up until we can stand on our own. And then we keep holding each other up anyway, because that's what love is."

Later that morning, Hope went back to Lily's room one more time. She opened the quote box and took out the card.

P.S. Say yes.

She tucked it carefully into her wallet, next to the "Stories save lives" card she'd been carrying for months.

Then she sat on Lily's bed, wrapped in her quilt, and looked around the room.

"I said yes," Hope told the air. "I'm choosing to be happy. I'm choosing to live. Just like you wanted."

The room stayed quiet, but Hope felt that familiar warmth. The steady reminder that love didn't end, it simply transformed.

Outside, the snow had stopped. The sun was breaking through the clouds, sending shafts of light through Lily's window. Good light, Lily would have called it. The kind that makes everything look possible.

Hope stood, smoothed the quilt, and went downstairs to where Sam was helping Rebecca make Christmas breakfast, where laughter filled the kitchen, where life continued its stubborn insistence on moving forward.

She paused in the doorway, watching Sam flip pancakes while Rebecca told him some story that had him laughing. Her phone buzzed in her pocket.

Jenna: *Merry Christmas! Can't stop thinking about last night. Lily would be so smug.*

Sheridan: *SO SMUG. But also, so happy. We're happy too. Love you.*

Hope smiled and texted back: *Love you both. Thank you for being there.*

She put her phone away and joined Sam and Rebecca in the kitchen, letting herself be pulled into the warmth, the noise, the messy beautiful reality of being alive and loved.

That afternoon, they'd drive back to La Crosse, back to the bookstore, back to the apartment with good light and a judgmental orange cat waiting.

Back home.

But for now, in this moment, Hope stood in the kitchen of the yellow Victorian and felt something she hadn't felt in a long time: Complete.

Not healed. Grief didn't work that way. She'd carry Lily with her always, in the ache that lived three inches to the left, in the quote cards tucked in her wallet, in the room upstairs that would stay exactly as it was.

But she'd also carry Sam. And Rebecca. And Jenna and Sheridan. And the bookstore and Book Rescue and every student who found the right words at the right time.

She'd carry all of it. The grief and the joy, the loss and the love, the past, and the future.

Because that's what Lily had taught her, in the end.

Stories save lives.

And this story, this one about wrong numbers and right people, about a mother learning to live again and a bookstore owner learning to love again, about a daughter who orchestrated a future she'd never see . . .

This story was saving them all.

THE END